Colter's Code

Colter's Code

Mark E. Uhler

Kindle Direct Publishing

Copyright © 2023 Mark E. Uhler
Jacket design by Kristian Koves
All rights reserved.
ISBN-13: 9798873064892
First edition

This is a work of fiction. Names, characters, places, and incidents either are the product of the author's imagination or are used fictitiously. Any resemblance to actual persons, living or dead, events, or locales is entirely coincidental.

For Justin and Jacob

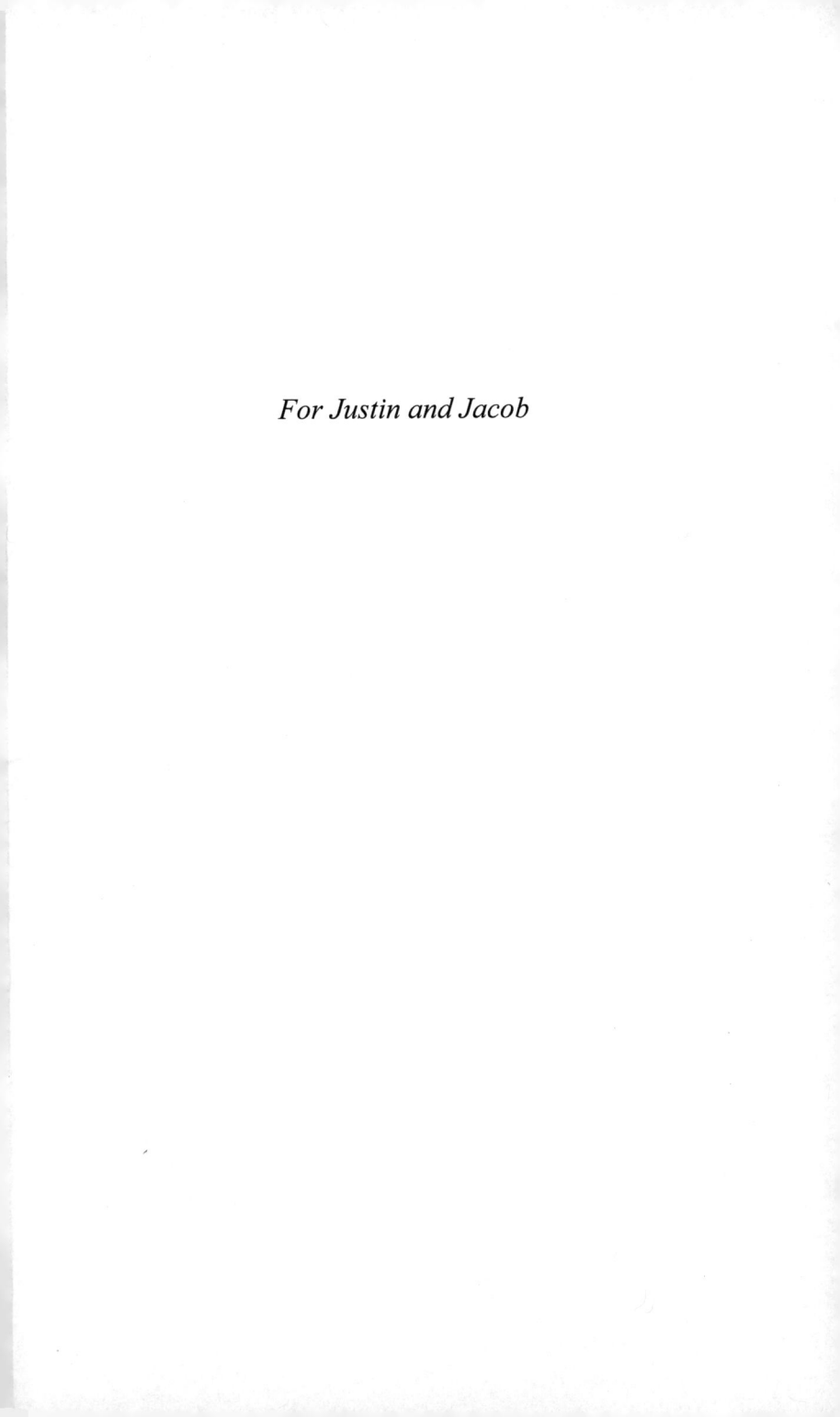

I'd like to acknowledge the skill and patience of my editors, who are dedicated to helping the imagination of others touch the written page:

Amy Megill
Chelsea Greenwood

Chapter 1
The Restaurant

John Colter was hiding in the dark shadows in an alley across the street from Sparks Restaurant, weighing the consequences of killing Sal Provenzano, a capo in the most powerful Mafia family in the United States. He knew the Genovese crime organization had unlimited power. The tentacles of their reach were everywhere, even in his hometown of Pittsburg, Kansas. He understood that killing a capo would be punished with extreme prejudice, but his code cried out for him to balance the scales of justice.

John had grown up in Maplewood, New Jersey, a suburb of New York City. Ever since he had been a child, television stations and newspapers sensationalized gangland murders as payment for any assault against the Mafia. He vividly remembered the image of a man in a barbershop chair in Brooklyn with his throat cut: bright-red blood was streaking down a white towel wrapped around his neck. The man was murdered as retribution for killing a member of the Genovese family.

John's first personal contact with the Mafia had occurred shortly after moving to the Midwest. He had stumbled into view of their power while visiting a friend in Kansas City. One of the most ruthless Mafia commission members, Carmine Civella, ruled Kansas City, and John's friend's father was a high-ranking member of the Civella family. One evening, the father invited his son and John on a tour of their underground tunnels. Starting in the basement, they explored an intricate maze of passageways connected to other Civella family members' houses, designed as a form of mutual protection. In one room called the armory, the father showed them machine guns, high-powered Browning automatic rifles, pistols, sawed-off shotguns, and thousands of rounds of ammunition. He bragged that they had more firepower than the Kansas City Police Department.

Closer to John's home, Crawford County was a renowned hub of whiskey manufacturing operations for the Mafia during Prohibition. Illegal booze was trucked to multiple northern cities as far away as Chicago. Bribes to local officials eliminated any government interference. Uncooperative residents were disappeared as fish food for the bass and crappie in the area's lakes that had been created by coal-mining strip pits. Local legend claimed that the county had more unsolved murders per capita than anywhere else in the United States.

Sal arrived at Sparks Restaurant at seven fifteen Wednesday night accompanied by two bodyguards and his girlfriend, Connie. John carefully watched the entourage enter the restaurant from his black tomb-like alley.

Sal was wearing a gray pinstriped Canali suit with a blue tie and black Armani shoes. Connie's sexy curves were accentuated by a tight dress and push-up bra that exposed more than half of her shapely breasts. The red Bergdorf Goodman hat she was wearing made her hair look like waves of white gold.

John sat watching, waiting for them to finish dinner and exit the restaurant. The minute hand on his watch moved like a turtle emerging from cold, deep waters. Tick. Tick. Tick. Doubt entered his mind: *Is this act of justice really worth the risk? If the Mafia finds out who I am, I'm a dead man. Debbie would understand the sacrifice. She's a strong woman. But what would she tell our children? Would they understand?* Then John pictured the two evil men walking out of the courtroom after the mistrial, mocking their accusers. They had believed they were above the law, untouchable.

John lived by a righteous code of honor that had limits of tolerance. Sal had crossed that line when he perverted the legal system to escape punishment for his crimes. John's muscles tensed with the resolve to right the wrong.

There he is. Sal was exiting the restaurant talking to his two bodyguards, Tony and Bruno. The adrenaline started pumping through his veins. *Take some deep breaths and calm down*, John told himself.

A Cuban cigar touched Sal's lips as he waited for Connie to finish her customary visit to the powder room. He was relishing the idea of an evening with

Connie alone in their apartment, dining on intimate pleasures. Bruno lit the cigar. The first puff was exhaled in a ring of smoke.

John's silhouette emerged from the shadows. He was disguised like a wino, wearing a putrid-smelling overcoat and crumpled, dirty hat. He carried a brown paper bag in his left hand concealing a half-full bottle of cheap wine. He had poured the other half down the front of the coat to create a repulsive stain. Adding to his masquerade, John hunched over as he ambled toward the three men, then staggered slightly into the street.

They watched in disgust.

Tony turned toward Sal and said, "Look at this bum. You want me to get him out of here before Connie comes out? This guy is revolting." Sal started to respond just as the wino slipped on a pair of sunglasses. The three confused men simultaneously thought, *That's odd, why is this guy putting on sunglasses at night?*

John drew closer and lurched like he was about to stumble. Then, he grabbed Sal's arm and whispered in his ear, "This is for Amy."

John dropped the flash-bang grenade on the ground. The quiet darkness exploded violently with a bright, blinding flash and an ear-piercing bang that disoriented Sal and the two bodyguards.

John withdrew his Smith & Wesson Model 19 revolver and shot Sal two times in the chest. The two hollow-point bullets with copper tips expanded after entry, tearing through the ribs and flesh on their path to the heart and lungs. John felt the scales of justice move toward balance with the weight of Sal's blood. A third shot to the forehead guaranteed the funeral.

John slipped the revolver back into his coat pocket and walked purposefully to the corner. There, he turned left down the street and entered a dark alley. A soft rain started falling, which helped to obscure his outline against the large dark-green trash container. He slipped off his coat, exposing a pair of blue jeans and a New York Jets football jersey. Then, he discarded the sunglasses, earplugs, and outer garments into a black plastic bag. They silently said hello to the other black bags waiting for their ocean swim. Turning, John looked up and down the alley. Finding no one in sight, he walked to the entrance, peeked around the corner, and casually walked away.

After the initial shock to the senses, Bruno and Tony regained their composure and inspected Sal's body, which was lying in a puddle of rain and blood. Bewilderment turned to anger.

Tony asked, "Did you see where that wino went?"

Bruno answered, "No. I didn't see or hear a thing after that flash thing. Did you?"

"We gotta find that motherfucker and kill his ass. You go that way. I'll go this way," Tony replied.

They withdrew their pistols and desperately searched the street to find the assassin. Tony headed west and stopped at the cross street. Bruno ran east down the long city block toward the Hudson River.

Tony found the broken wine bottle wrapped in a torn brown paper bag around the corner on the Third Avenue sidewalk. Then he found the alley. At the entrance, he paused and pointed his gun inward, searching for any movement. Looking intently into the shadows, he noticed only a dumpster. *Where the hell is this guy?* he asked himself.

Meanwhile, to the east, Bruno saw two men wearing black raincoats and hats. He eliminated them as suspects after closer investigation and resumed the hunt down Second Avenue. *Wait. There. Is that him?* He noticed a man getting into a yellow cab. *No. The wino didn't have a beard. That's not him.*

Then, two young girls walked toward him under an umbrella. *Damn*, he said to himself, *there's no wino in sight.*

Slowly, Bruno's anger changed to the realization that he had failed. Dejected, he walked back to the restaurant.

Tony, on the other hand, was excited. He noticed a man similar in size to the wino walking away. He ran to catch the guy, yelling, "Hey, you, stop right there!"

Colter's Code

The startled man stopped and turned around to identify the source of the command. Tony was running straight at him, waving a large handgun. The man raised his hands in submission, hoping to appear nonthreatening. It didn't help.

Tony closed the gap; he was about to capture the wino. *I've got you now, you fucker. I'll take you back to Angelo and I'll be the hero*, he dreamed.

He aimed his pistol at the man's forehead. "Who the hell are you?" Tony shouted—as he realized the guy was not the wino.

The frightened little old man's wet, green coat only looked like the one the wino had been wearing.

John's pace to escape slowed to allow a well-dressed couple walking in the same direction to catch up. As they approached, he said, "How are you folks this fine evening?"

The woman answered, "We just enjoyed dinner at the 21 Club and a show at Rockefeller Center."

John looked back and noticed one of the bodyguards was following them.

"I wonder if you could help me out. I am looking for the nearest subway station." He knew the answer but wanted to appear to blend in with the couple.

The women offered, "Well, we're walking that way. Come with us and we'll show you."

Tony looked down the street and noticed an older couple talking to a guy wearing a Jets football jersey and Jets hat. Tony wondered, *Is that the guy?* Then decided, *No, that's not him.* Exasperated, he said to himself, *Where is this goddamn wino?*

Two blocks later, John thanked the couple and disappeared into the subway station.

Having failed to find the assassin, Tony holstered his pistol and returned to the restaurant. By now, the police had arrived and sealed off the crime scene. From across the street, he telephoned Angelo Galante, the underboss of the Genovese crime family. An associate answered the phone and said, "This is Dominic. Can I help you?"

"Yeah, Dominic, this is Tony. I need to talk to Angelo right away."

Angelo grabbed the phone and said, "Tony. Angelo. What's up?"

Tony answered, "I've got some bad news. Sal was just hit in front of Sparks."

Angelo replied in a stern voice, "Did you get the shooters?"

Tony paused, knowing his answer would have dire consequences, then said, "No: we chased him, but he got away."

Angelo's eyes turned black like coal, his cheeks erupted red, the veins in his neck popped out like balloons, and he shouted into the telephone, "What the hell do you mean, you let him get away?"

Tony answered with trepidation, "This guy came out of nowhere dressed like a wino and stumbled toward us. He seemed harmless at first. Suddenly there was this bright flash and loud explosion. We couldn't see or hear anything. When we gained our senses, Sal was lying on the sidewalk, dead. Bruno and I looked up and down the street but didn't see the guy, so we searched and searched—but the guy just disappeared."

Angelo barked, "Where's Bruno?"

"He's with Connie."

"All right. You get her out of there. Take her back to Sal's apartment. We don't want her talking to anyone. You got that? Stay with her until I send someone over to babysit her. Tell Bruno to get over here right now!"

Angelo began compiling a mental list of enemies who wanted to kill Sal Provenzano and had the balls to do it. He also wondered, *If a rival family did this, that explains not killing the girlfriend*—the Mafia's code prohibited killing her—*but why not kill Tony and Bruno? What kind of assassin doesn't kill the bodyguards?*

Bruno arrived.

"Tell me step-by-step what happened. I want every detail," Angelo demanded.

Bruno described as much as possible as he watched the rage emanating from Angelo. "This guy dressed like a drunken bum walks up to us, and suddenly my eyes are blinded by a bright flash, like a camera bulb going off, and kablam! I don't remember what happened after that. When I came to, I saw Sal dead on the sidewalk. Tony and I looked around, and the guy was gone. We searched the neighborhood but couldn't find him. He just vanished like a ghost."

Angelo thought Bruno's story was consistent with Tony's phone call, but couldn't stop thinking to himself, *That still doesn't explain why the shooter didn't kill you and Tony.*

Back at the apartment, Tony was relieved by an associate, and he drove to meet Angelo. *Angelo sure was mad*, he thought as he sped through the rainy night. *As volatile as he is, no tellin' what he's going to do to Bruno and me. Maybe I should just get the hell out of here. I can pick up my stash of guns and money on my way out of town.* He paused, thinking. *If I leave, it will send a message to Angelo that I was in on it. Then what? Hell, there's nowhere to escape anyway. Angelo's people will hunt me down, and then the pain and suffering will be unbearable. Only my death would end it—and what about my family? My family! Shit, he'll kill them too.*

Angelo's temper reached its boiling point as Tony arrived. He fumed at his limp answers. *He's really pissin' me off*, he thought to himself. *How the hell did these two heavily armed idiots just let Sal's killer walk away? I should beat this fucker to death on principle.*

The intense questioning yielded little useful information to discover the assassin's motive and identity. Piecing together the two stories, Angelo concluded the guy was skilled with a handgun, quick and efficient. After analyzing everything they said, Angelo decided the flash thing was a solid lead. He called Detective Miller in the Newark Police Department.

Miller listened empathetically, sensing Angelo's rage in the tone of his voice. He understood not to mess with Angelo Galante. Then he said, "Angelo, what you described sounds like something SWAT uses in extreme situations. I don't know that much about them, but I know a guy who does. I'll ask him to call you right away."

The sergeant who answered Big Al Jones's telephone said he was out investigating a crime scene. He gave Miller Al's pager number.

Six-foot-four, two hundred eighty-pound Big Al lumbered over to a nearby payphone and called the pager number shown on the screen.

"Hey, Al, this is Detective Miller. Thanks for calling me back so quickly. I need a solid here, and a big one. Sal Provenzano was murdered tonight in front of Sparks Restaurant."

Al's raspy voice answered, "Yeah, I heard that on the radio. Let's hope it doesn't start another war between the families. We still haven't cleared all the murders from the last one."

"Well, a mutual friend of ours, Angelo Galante, called me asking questions about some kind of explosive device the attacker used to stun Provenzano and the two bodyguards before shooting Provenzano. What Angelo described sounds like a flash-bang grenade. Can you give Angelo a call and help him out? I'll give you his number."

Al wrote it down in his notebook. Then he inserted a few more coins in the payphone and called the number. "This is Al Jones with the Newark Police Department. Detective Miller asked me to give Mr. Galante a call."

Angelo scurried to the phone and said, "This is Angelo." Al's heartbeat elevated hearing his gruff voice. He knew Angelo was rumored to be a member of the Black Hand, a secret society of the most feared killers in the Mafia. Even psychopaths like the cold-blooded Mafia assassin known as "The Iceman" avoided the society's wrath. The Hand's prolific skill at brutal torture and stealth-like murders was legendary, only evidenced when they occasionally left their calling card: a black handprint near the victims.

"Mr. Galante," said Al. "Detective Miller asked me to call you to answer some questions you had about some kind of explosive device?"

Angelo described what happened then asked, "You ever heard of anything like that?"

"Yes, sir, It's called a flash-bang grenade. Unlike a standard military hand grenade that explodes, sending metal fragments designed to kill or maim the enemy, its designed not to kill the targets. Instead, the grenade explodes with a bright flash that temporarily blinds the victims for about ten seconds. Another devastating effect is that it creates a sonic shockwave, causing disorientation in the subjects. I'm not sure how exactly the science works, but it does something bad to the inner ear. The victims become deaf, get dizzy, and are totally disoriented. I started using them when I was a Green Beret in Vietnam. The British SAS invented them, and today, the military and police departments all over the United States use them for special tactical situations to stun people. Let me describe an example of how SWAT uses them here in Newark. Before our SWAT team enters a hostile environment, like a house full of dangerous criminals where one of us could be killed, we throw a flash-bang grenade through the door to neutralize anyone on the other side. It doesn't kill anyone, but they're totally disoriented."

Angelo curiously asked, "Don't you SWAT guys get blinded by the light and disoriented from the explosion?"

"No, sir. We wear special goggles like sunglasses and ear protection along with our helmets and body armor. When we enter the room, sometimes the victims' ears and noses are bleeding from the intense sound wave. If someone is holding a gun, we just shoot them before they recover their senses. It's great for hostage rescue situations."

Angelo responded, "Where the hell do you get those things?"

"That, I don't know. We just requisition our equipment through our captain. But let me do some checking around and call you back."

Angelo said, "Thanks. Get back to me as soon as you find out something. I'll make sure you receive a thicker envelope."

"Yes, sir, I'll get on it right away."

A few minutes later, Philip Castellano, the godfather of the family, walked into the room and asked Angelo for a status report. Once Angelo had finished, Castellano thought to himself, *Who would have a beef with Sal worth killing him over?*

Then he wondered, *Maybe another New York family killed him. But would they take that kind of risk?* He didn't think that was a possibility, but he wasn't sure.

If not one of the other four families, who was it? Maybe it was that African American gang over in Newark. We're always fighting over turf and killing some low-level soldiers. But killing one of my capos? They're not that stupid. Or are they?

***

Once John was confident that he had eluded the two bodyguards using the maze of underground subway trains, he exited at the Bowling Green station in Lower Manhattan. As an added precaution, he meandered north in the opposite direction. Then, he ducked into a storefront and watched for anyone who might have followed.

Starving after his adrenaline rush, John bought a hot coffee with cream and an Entenmann's coffee cake at the Staten Island Ferry Terminal. A few minutes later, he boarded the ferryboat and watched the white sea foam lick the stern as seagulls sang their songs of discovery.

The ferryboat crept away from the dock, gaining speed across the bay. John watched the tall buildings slowly fade to miniature silhouettes again the dark sky as the boat sped past the Statue of Liberty. The statue reminded John of his Norwegian grandparents coming to America with the dream of a better life for their children. They understood the price paid for freedom, as evidenced by the four blue stars on the red-and-white banner hanging in their living room window during World War II. Their four boys had served to protect the United States from evil men in Germany and Japan who wanted to dominate the world.

Now, John was fighting a different kind of war against evil men. This time, the battlefields were in New York City and the war was against the Mafia, who ruled with the same kind of oppression and murder.

John felt at peace believing his righteous kill had his grandparents' blessing while he ate a slice of the cake and sipped his coffee. Then he slipped the Smith & Wesson pistol and unused ammunition into the coffee cake's brown bag. He inched closer to the boat's railing and casually dropped the bag into the murky waters while his fellow passengers were mesmerized looking back at the lights of Downtown Manhattan stamped against the dark sky. Fifteen minutes later, in St. George, John rode the last train to Tottenville at the end of the line.

There it is, he thought to himself, *21 Hoppling Avenue.* He smiled as Margret and Betty greeted John with big hugs and kisses. The Browns were old family friends. They owned a house on Staten Island a few blocks from the Tottenville train station.

Margret asked, "How was your evening in the city?"

"I had delicious lasagna and meatballs at Joe's Restaurant. It's always too much food but a special treat." He left out the part about taking a subway detour to Sparks Restaurant to kill Sal Provenzano.

"I see you're wearing a Jets football jersey and hat. You always did love the Jets. I remember how excited you were when you met Broadway Joe. Joe Namath was so handsome," Margret said.

The next morning at breakfast, Margret asked, "Did you read the paper this morning? That mobster fella who killed Amy was found shot to death outside of a restaurant in the city last night. He finally got what he deserved."

John sipped his coffee. "Was anyone else hurt?"

"No, just the mob guy."

John thought to himself, *Sal chose to live by a code of evil. He believed that he had escaped justice. Not this time—righteousness prevailed.* "Do the police know who killed him?" he asked.

Margret responded, "The paper said the police have no clues and no witnesses. Apparently, some kind of bomb exploded, distracting everyone."

She shifted subjects, adding, "Did you know your grandfather made bombs during World War I? He told me part of the White Manufacturing Plant where I worked all those years as his secretary was converted into making dynamite for artillery shells. You always enjoyed time with your grandfather doing those chemistry experiments together. Say, didn't the two of you make dynamite once?"

He answered, "Yes. Grampa showed me how to make all kinds of explosive devices."

Mark E. Uhler

John had completed the first mission in his one-man war against the Mafia. Now, it was time to return to his loving family in Kansas.

Chapter 2
The Van

It was a peaceful sunny morning when Salvatore Provenzano sauntered out his front door to retrieve the August 20, 1975, edition of the *Star-Ledger* newspaper. On the way, Sal noticed a black van parked across the street with the name "Ferrante Plumbing" painted in large white letters on the side. He glanced up and down the street of his Maplewood, New Jersey, neighborhood, looking for the repairman. He didn't see anyone, so he went inside to resume his daily routine of reading the paper while sipping his espresso. Today, he had a special treat: a delicious cream-filled Ferrara's Bakery cannoli. Sal loved eating cannoli and had the waistline to prove it.

But he couldn't stop thinking about that van. His level of interest rose, and he walked to the living room window to look again. No one was in sight. As time passed without activity, his curiosity changed to apprehension.

Sal lived in a world based on suspicion and violence to survive. He had received promotions in the Genovese crime family from associate, to soldier, to capo. The rewards provided the money to move his family from a congested, dirty Brooklyn, New York, neighborhood to Maplewood. They relished the lifestyle in the affluent suburbs with green grass and beautiful tall trees.

His neighbors knew Sal was in the Mafia, but to them, he appeared to be a handsome, friendly businessman. They didn't know about his evil, dark side, that he was a cold, calculating killer with a history of ruthless, violent murders.

***

Sal's rise to power in the Mafia had begun in 1948 when he heard the old beige rotary phone ring on the kitchen wall.

He answered the phone. It was his boss, Angelo Galante, one of the capos.

"Sal. This is Angelo. Pick me up in thirty minutes. We got a job to do for Phil."

Sal answered, "I'm on my way. Do I need any special equipment?"

"No. Just the usual," Angelo replied. He knew Sal packed a Smith & Wesson 19 wherever he went, and in the trunk of his car, he had two Remington Model 870 pump-action shotguns with enough ammunition to fight off a small army.

Sal drove his black 1946 Ford Super Deluxe two-door coupe to meet Angelo, and together they traveled to South Orange, New Jersey, for a job involving a hit on Vincent Campisi.

Campisi was operating an auto repair business used by the Genovese crime syndicate as a lucrative chop shop to disassemble stolen cars for resale. Tensions had percolated over time between Campisi and Marco DeMeo, the underboss of the northern New Jersey territory. It was simple, really. DeMeo demanded more money, and Campisi withheld the increase from the weekly envelope. In response to the blatant disobedience, DeMeo sent his minions to collect and Campisi reluctantly paid. But then, as the feud escalated, Campisi made a fatal mistake. He contacted the Essex County District Attorney's office, and he agreed to testify against DeMeo in exchange for immunity and safety in the federal witness protection program.

That afternoon, DeMeo had received a tip about Campisi's betrayal from an auto crimes detective on the Genovese payroll. DeMeo was furious and ordered Angelo to kill the rat.

Campisi surmised DeMeo would put out a hit order on him for his betrayal, and he went into hiding. He was right. DeMeo spread the word throughout the organization that any information about Campisi's whereabouts would be handsomely rewarded. Within hours, a Genovese family associate located Campisi's hideout at his girlfriend's apartment in South Orange.

Sal and Angelo waited across the street until they noticed Campisi walking down the sidewalk. As Campisi turned to walk up the concrete steps to the front porch, Sal and Angelo stopped him and then forced him into their car at gunpoint. They drove Campisi to a nearby butcher shop, stabbed him repeatedly with a butcher's knife, and decapitated him. The next day, the cleaning staff at the courthouse were horrified when they discovered a headless body in a dumpster. Inside the courthouse, the District Attorney's office understood the message.

Sal killed the man without emotion or remorse—he never cared about ending someone's life. He returned home after the vicious murder, entered his sleeping daughter's bedroom, and kissed her goodnight on the cheek. Then Sal walked down the hallway into Joey's bedroom, kissed him on the forehead, and softly whispered, "Sleep well, my son." Sal slept peacefully next to his wife, Carla. To him, it had just been another job.

***

Sal finished his espresso and walked to the back of the house.

"Hey, Joey. Come up here for a minute!" he yelled down the basement stairway.

Joey interrupted his telephone conversation with an associate and said, "I'll call you back. My dad needs me upstairs."

He found Sal staring out the living room window and asked, "What's up, Pop?"

Sal answered, "Do you see that black van across the street? It's just been sitting out there. Have you ever seen that van before?"

Joey replied, "No. Why do you ask?"

"I've been watching that van since I went out to get the paper this morning. I haven't seen anyone go in or out of it."

Joey said, "That's odd. You want me to call a couple of guys?"

Sal scoffed. "We can handle this ourselves."

Sal's suspicion was that the van posed a potential threat because of a recent turf war that had erupted in Newark over drug-dealer boundaries. A rival African American organized-crime group called The Family had been exercising their muscle by expanding into the Genovese family's territory. During the turf battle, The Family had brutally murdered a DeMeo soldier and two associates. As retaliation, DeMeo had ordered his crew to kill any Family member trespassing in Genovese territory. The bullet-riddled bodies of four Family crew members had been found on street corners. The funeral business was booming in Newark.

As the hours passed, the tension in the living room began to build like a geyser in Yellowstone. Sal's paranoid imagination projected the picture of two men leaping out of the van's back doors as he backed his black Cadillac sedan down the driveway. One attacker would shoot him in the head. At the same time, a partner would circle around to the passenger side and kill Joey.

Sal had murdered unsuspecting victims in their driveways more than once using sawed-off shotguns.

Yes, he thought to himself, *that's the perfect killing spot. That's what I would do.*

Sal had an idea. He grabbed the telephone and called the number painted on the van. No ringing. A recorded voice answered, "The number you have dialed is no longer in service." The tension reached critical mass. Sal was a psychopath capable of committing heinous acts of violence. He didn't hear a benevolent voice in his head whispering, *Don't kill the people in the van. Call the police. They will handle it.*

Sal looked at Joey and said, "Come with me. We're going to kill those fuckers in the van before they get us."

They retrieved two pump-action Mossberg twelve-gauge shotguns from the black steel gun safe in the basement. For maximum firepower, they loaded the shotguns with double-aught buckshot. Upstairs, Sal smashed his living room window with the butt of the gun, creating an unobstructed line of fire.

They both opened fire at the same time, sending buckshot at over 1,300 feet per second into the van. Red flames and black gunpowder leaped out of the shotgun barrels like fire bellowing out of the mouth of an angry dragon. They reloaded and fired again. The loud blasts coming from their house reached a deafening crescendo. The force of the gray lead pellets ripped apart the van and neutralized the threat.

In the mayhem, errant shots penetrated the Colter house across the street. They perforated the red shingle exterior walls and shattered the glass window of the downstairs bedroom.

The pungent smell of gunpowder danced around Sal and Joey as they triumphantly walked out the front door to find the dead assassins. They thought to themselves, *No one could have lived through a lead wall of destruction like that one.*

They cautiously drew closer and opened the back doors. The van was empty. Feeling foolish that they had overreacted, Sal and Joey nonchalantly returned to the house acting like nothing happened.

Sal broke the silence. "Better to be safe than make a mistake that gets us killed."

Then, he dialed his lawyer.

A secretary answered, "Hello, Frank Lautenberg's office."

Sal said, "This is Sal Provenzano. Let me speak to Frank right away. It's an urgent matter."

A moment later, Frank picked up the phone. "Hi, Sal. What's this urgent matter?"

"Come over to my house right away. We thought we were getting hit by some guys waiting in a van parked outside the house. We shot the hell out of it and when we went to check it out, it was empty."

Frank answered, "Understood. I'll be right over."

Next, Sal dialed one of his soldiers. "Bruno, this is Sal. Get over to my house right away. I have a job for you."

Chapter 3
Amy's Room

Linda Colter was standing in the kitchen making dinner when she heard loud bangs outside followed by the sound of breaking glass. After a pause, she heard more loud bangs, then popping noises coming from the kitchen walls. *What was that?* she wondered. Small black objects whistled past her head, piercing the still air. Instinctively, she ducked down in alarm.

Linda realized something was terribly wrong when Max suddenly stopped barking downstairs. Her confusion turned to powerful resolve as she yelled, "Amy, are you OK?"

No answer.

Her heart raced. She shouted again, "Amy, Amy, are you OK?"

Silence, then panic.

Nine-year-old Amy had been cheerfully playing downstairs on her bedroom carpet. The sweet sound of her singing a favorite children's song suddenly stopped when strange noises engulfed her room. Sparkling glass fragments rained down as buckshot pellets whizzed by her.

Linda bolted down the stairs, and terror was waiting for her when she entered the room. She found Amy lying motionless on the floor holding Lammy, her stuffed white lamb. Max, her faithful Labrador, lay motionless beside her. The pink window curtains fluttered softly in the air from a gentle breeze passing through the broken glass. Then Linda noticed red and pinkish spots on Amy's yellow dress. She screamed in panic.

"Oh my god! Oh my god!" Frantically, she knelt beside her daughter for a closer look and noticed a red blotch on Amy's temple. She gently slipped one arm under Amy's head. Her hair was wet and gooey in the back. Linda gasped for air, her heart wrenching in more pain than it had on that day a soldier dressed in full ceremonial uniform knocked on the front door. He had brought the devastating news that her husband, Jack, had been killed in Vietnam.

Next door, neighbor Henry Carlson heard the gunshots and cautiously walked outside to find their origin. Faint sounds of crying resonated from a broken downstairs window at the Colters' house. He ran to the front door to investigate and opened it. *That's odd*, he thought. *Where's Max? That dog always greets me.* He found Linda downstairs in Amy's bedroom. She was in shock and sitting on the floor, gently rocking Amy. He discovered why Max hadn't rambunctiously greeted him upstairs.

Carlson empathetically said, "Linda, let me help you with Amy," then he knelt beside her to examine Amy's wounds. He felt a weak pulse and noticed shallow breathing. He discovered that the bleeding had stopped, but he knew Amy needed immediate medical attention.

He asked, "Linda, did you call an ambulance?"
She stuttered, "No, no. Not yet."
"Where is your telephone?"

Linda never remembered the events after lifting Amy into her arms that day. To heal her shattered heart, her mind locked the painful memories into a deep, dark chamber.

***

Across the street, Mrs. Emma Walker, an eighty-one-year-old neighbor, had been drinking her afternoon tea when she heard loud bangs outside like a car backfiring. *I wonder what that could be*, she said to herself as she hobbled out of her old comfy chair to the living room window. There, she noticed a black van parked in the street. *Why is the driver's-side window broken? I better go outside for a closer look*, she thought. Suddenly, as she stood on the porch studying the van, more gunshot blasts erupted from the neighbors' house. She turned toward the Provenzanos' in time to witness fiery flashes leaping out from the front window. Buckshot whistled through the air like little black flies, followed by the sound of popping coming from the van.

Mrs. Walker's heart was pounding. She scurried back into her house for safety saying, "Oh, my goodness. Oh, my goodness." In her anxiety, she called the police.

Mark E. Uhler

A women answered, "Hello. This is the Maplewood Police Department. May I help you?"

Mrs. Walker said in a frightened, stammering voice, "There are gunshots coming out of my neighbor's house."

"Ma'am, please take a deep breath and slowly exhale. Try to calm down. What is your name?"

"My name is Emma Walker."

"And where do you live, Mrs. Walker?"

"I live at 179 Norfolk Street in Maplewood, just off Parker."

"What's the name of your neighbor's where the gunshots are coming from, and what is the address?"

"Sal Provenzano. You know, the mob guy. His street address is 181 Norfolk. The big white house. You can't miss it. Mine is the red house next to it."

"How do you know the gunshots are coming from Mr. Provenzano's house?"

"Well, when I heard the first loud bangs, I was curious, so I looked out the living room window. I didn't see anything and went outside onto my front porch. That's when I heard more awful loud bangs. It was very scary. I looked over at the Provenzanos' and saw flaming stuff coming from inside the house."

"OK. Mrs. Walker, I want you to stay in a safe place in your house. We'll send a patrol car over right away. Thank you for your help. I'm going to hang up now and get this to dispatch."

Colter's Code

The desk clerk gave the intake form to the dispatch operator and described Mrs. Walker's alarming call.

Across town, Officer Connolly answered the radio: "Dispatch. This is Officer Connolly. Go ahead."

The operator said, "We have a report of gunshots fired at 181 Norfolk. Can you respond?"

"Ten-four. We're on our way."

Back at the Provenzano residence, Sal and Joey decided to eliminate any evidence. First, they picked up the empty shell casings in the living room and deposited them in a brown Acme grocery shopping bag. A half-empty box of shotguns shells joined them.

After they finished the cleanup, Joey left through the back door.

Bruno knocked fifteen minutes later.

Sal answered and handed him the two Mossberg shotguns and the brown paper bag and said, "You know what to do. Make these disappear."

Officers Bill Wagner and Patrick Connolly parked their patrol car in front of the big white house at 181 Norfolk Avenue.

Connolly said, "Isn't that Sal Provenzano's house?"

Wagner answered, "Yes, it is. We better be careful on this one. He's not the kind of guy you want to piss off."

As they looked around the neighborhood, Wagner said, "What the hell. Do you see that?" He pointed to the van. "We better go check it out." Moments later, they noticed that the panel wall was peppered with bullet holes.

They withdrew their Colt Police Positive .38 Special revolvers and cautiously approached the van.

Wagner shouted, "This is the police. Is anyone in there?"

No answer.

He slowly turned the handle and opened the door while Connolly pointed his revolver inward.

Connolly said, "I don't see anyone inside." He pulled out his flashlight to search for any clues then said, "I don't see any blood or any evidence that anyone was in the van during the shooting."

Wagner replied, "I wonder what happened here?"

The patrolmen stepped back from the van and started searching the neighborhood.

Connolly was the first to notice the broken window at the Colters' house and said, "Hey, Wagner. Look over at that house. The downstairs window is broken. Let's go see if it's related."

As they walked closer, they noticed black round spots all over the front of the house.

Wagner said, "Those look like bullet holes."

Connolly knocked. An older man answered.

Wagner took the lead. "Hi. This is Officer Connolly, and I'm Officer Wagner. We're with the Maplewood Police Department. We received a

Colter's Code

telephone call from one of the neighbors who reported they heard gunshots. Can you give us your name and tell us what happened here?"

Carlson responded, "My name is Henry Carlson, and I live next door." He pointed in the direction of his house.

Connolly interjected, "Then what are you doing in this house?"

Carlson answered, "Well, I was watching the Yankees game when I heard gunshots outside and decided to find out what the hell was going on. So, I got up and went outside. That's when I saw Sal and Joey shooting their shotguns at that van."

Wagner asked, "How do you know they were shotguns?"

Carlson replied, "I was a Marine on Guadalcanal during World War II. Believe me, I know what shotguns look like and sound like. When the gunfire stopped, I heard the faint sound of crying coming from the downstairs window of this house, the Colters' house. That's when I came over here and knocked on the front door. No one answered, so I turned the doorknob, and it was unlocked. I opened it, then yelled, 'Linda, is everyone all right in there? This is Mr. Carlson.' When no one answered, I went downstairs and found Mrs. Colter in her daughter's bedroom. She was crying and rocking Amy. Amy was shot and her wounds were pretty serious, so I called for an ambulance. They said they're on their way. Come with me; I'll show you."

Carlson guided Connolly and Wagner to Amy's bedroom, where they found Linda sitting on the blood-stained, beige carpet sobbing and holding her daughter. Connolly was suddenly overcome at the sight of a little girl's flesh, bone, and brain matter splattered over the floor. He was a father of two young daughters and became nauseated. His facial expression signaled what was coming next. He held his mouth tightly and suddenly raced out of the house to vomit. Nightmares recalling the images of the gruesome scene haunted him for years.

Wagner followed his partner outside. "You OK, partner? It was pretty bad in there."

Connolly wiped his mouth and responded, "I'll be all right. Give me a minute."

Wagner called dispatch. "This is Wagner. There's a little girl here with multiple gunshot wounds. Can you send some detectives? We're going to need help on this one. Oh, and an ambulance is in route. Can you check the status?"

Dispatch answered, "Hold on while I radio the ambulance." A minute later the radio clicked on: "The ambulance is almost there."

The soft sounds of distant sirens grew louder. Connolly waited outside to direct the paramedics downstairs to Amy's bedroom. Carol Wilson and John

Van Buren brought the gurney while Connolly carried the medical supply bag.

Carol softly said, "Mrs. Colter. My name is Carol Wilson, and this is my partner, John Van Buren. We're here to help your daughter. What's her name?"

Linda turned to the voice coming from the object standing next to her. Her bloodshot eyes telegraphed her fear and pain. "Her name is Amy."

Carol responded, "Linda, I need to examine Amy: is that OK?"

Linda was numb from shock and slowly nodded her approval. Carol found four bullet holes. The pellet that hit Amy's head had exited out the other side, leaving her hair matted with dried red blood. Carol carefully turned Amy on her side. There, she found three thumbnail-sized holes in her back. She had a weak pulse, and her blood pressure was critically low. Carol reached into her medical bag and pulled out a stethoscope. The gurgling sound in Amy's lungs elevated Carol's concern. She completed the triage and dressed the wounds with temporary bandages.

Van Buren placed an oxygen mask over Amy's mouth to help increase the blood oxygen levels. Next, he inserted an intravenous line into her arm to start the flow of vital fluids.

Chapter 4
The Detectives

Detectives Robert O'Keefe and Shaun Murphy arrived at the crime scene and asked the senior patrolman Wagner for a summary of the incident.

Wagner responded, "All hell broke loose when two men fired shotguns from that house over there"—he pointed to the Provenzanos'—"at this van. Some of the pellets missed the van, penetrated the walls of the Colters' house, and hit a little girl named Amy Colter while she was playing in her bedroom. The paramedics are downstairs helping her right now."

O'Keefe looked back at 181 Norfolk and thought, *Damn, Sal Provenzano lives there. He's a ruthless son of a bitch.* O'Keefe asked, "Did you talk to anyone at the Provenzano house?"

Wagner responded, "No, sir. That's above our pay grade. We waited for you guys."

The ambulance raced to the trauma center at College Hospital in Newark. On the way, Van Buren radioed ahead that the patient was in critical condition. She was a nine-year-old girl who had sustained multiple gunshot wounds. Inside the box, Carol's concern grew as Amy's condition deteriorated. The crackling sound in her chest was more pronounced because fluids were filling up her lungs and restricting the oxygen she needed to sustain her life. Without alarming Linda, who was sitting next to her, Carol replaced the oxygen mask with a breathing bag mask and started squeezing the reservoir to force air into Amy's lungs. Time was running out.

Back at the crime scene, O'Keefe was on the hunt for witnesses. He said to the patrolmen, "Murphy and I will interview Provenzano, Mrs. Walker, and Mr. Carlson. I want you two to canvas the rest of the neighborhood."

The doorbell rang and Mrs. Farrell answered, "Hello, officers. May I help you?"

Connolly replied, "Yes, ma'am. We're with the Maplewood Police Department. We're investigating a shooting down the street. Did you hear or see anything unusual in the neighborhood in the last few hours?"

She replied, "No, officer. I was eating lunch in the kitchen, and after that, I was sewing in the back bedroom. I didn't hear a thing."

Wagner asked, "Is anyone else home?"

Mrs. Farrell answered, "No. My husband, David, is at the Jersey Shore fishing with some friends."

Connolly wrote her name and address in his pocket notebook, and they resumed their inquiries. A garage door opened as they walked toward the next house. Wagner started waving his arms and yelling to get the driver's attention.

Mr. Wyatt rolled down his window and said, "What's the matter, officers?"

Wagner responded, "We're investigating a shooting a few doors down from yours. Did you see anything unusual or hear any loud noises?"

Mr. Wyatt answered, "No, sir. I didn't see a thing. I was in the house until just now. I'm leaving to go to the A&P to buy some groceries. As far as hearing anything"—he shrugged his shoulders—"my hearing isn't so good anymore. I drove a bulldozer for over twenty years."

A police photographer arrived to memorialize the day's mayhem. First, he snapped pictures in the Colters' kitchen, highlighting the beams of light shining through the round holes in the walls that illuminated the dust particles meandering through the air. In Amy's bedroom, he captured images of the broken window and the once-still curtains, now waving like flags. He flinched in horror when the camera lens focused on the blood-spattered bedspread. And again at the sight of the brownish-red puddle of dried blood stained into the carpet. He wondered, *What kind of monster would do this to an innocent little girl?* It was his first week on the job. He had a sister Amy's age.

To contrast the brutality of the crime scene, he photographed the serenity of her light-brown teddy bear sitting on a small wooden chair, staring through its black button eyes. He turned to the left wall: flash, click.

A frame recorded the image of a math textbook parked on the desk, ready to share exercises in addition, subtraction, multiplication, and division. Another frame captured a pink lamp wearing a white shade that stood ready to brighten the activities of a little girl's playful day.

In the street, he recorded images of the ravaged van. Inside, a special twenty-four-millimeter lens captured the pellet-riddled black seats and pieces of white seat-cushion stuffing scattered throughout the cabin.

In the meantime, Detectives O'Keefe and Murphy approached the Provenzano house. A man wearing gold-rimmed spectacles and a perfectly tailored suit answered the knock at the front door. "May I help you gentlemen?" he said in a regal voice.

Sal stood behind him holding a glass of Macallan 18 and took a swig.

O'Keefe answered in surprise, "Who are you?"

He replied, "I'm Mr. Provenzano's attorney, Frank Lautenberg."

Irritated that Provenzano's attorney was present, O'Keefe said, "Mr. Provenzano, my name is Detective Robert O'Keefe, and this is Detective Shaun Murphy. We're with the Maplewood Police Department. We would like to ask you some questions about what happened here today. May we come in the house?"

Lautenberg answered, "Detectives, Mr. Provenzano is willing to answer your questions, but unfortunately, today's events were very upsetting. To calm his nerves, he drank a few glasses of Scotch. We'll have to arrange for a subsequent interview. In answer to your request to enter Mr. Provenzano's residence, may I ask if you have a search warrant?"

Getting frustrated, O'Keefe responded, "No, sir, we don't."

Lautenberg said, "Well, then. Mr. Provenzano respectfully declines your request to enter his house."

O'Keefe stood gritting his teeth.

Lautenberg knew once he informed the detectives that Sal was drinking alcohol, any questions asked and answered after that were inadmissible in court. "Is there anything else, detectives?" he said.

O'Keefe reluctantly said, "I guess we're done for now. We'll be back with a search warrant."

Lautenberg handed O'Keefe his business card, saying, "Call me tomorrow to arrange an interview with Mr. Provenzano. We'll be happy to accommodate your request and answer your questions at that time."

***

The code Sal lived by was the antithesis of John Colter's. Sal's way of life rewarded those who used fear, intimidation, bullying, bribery, and ruthless murder as tools to take what they wanted when they wanted it. Their code glamorized stealing, worshipped money, and ruthlessly punished anyone who opposed them.

Every Wednesday, Sal stayed in New York City with his lover Connie Aiello, the goombah. For a love shack, he rented a two-bedroom apartment three blocks from Times Square in the Theater District. Connie loved living luxuriously, especially shopping at Bergdorf Goodman, Bloomingdale's, and Saks Fifth Avenue.

As a façade, Sal held a position as a vice president of the International Brotherhood of Teamsters in Newark, New Jersey, to mask his illegal activities in the dark shadows of society, but his real money came from gambling, prostitution, extortion, and kickbacks from construction companies.

One of Sal's favorite and most profitable businesses was operating a numbers racket, an illegal lottery typically located in local grocery stores in poor, working-class neighborhoods. Stores like Joe's Candy Store on Market Street, with a steady stream of families and children. They were the perfect fronts for the Mafia's gambling operations because they blended in with established businesses. Bettors, the gamblers, selected three numbers and placed a bet with the bookmaker, the "bookie," hoping to be the lucky person who correctly picked the three winning numbers. Joey supervised the operation and hired local youth called "runners" to transport the cash and betting slips to a central location called "the bank." The following day, the Mafia's "banker" randomly selected the winning numbers, and the holders of the ticket with those numbers received a fixed payment of cash.

A similar lucrative gambling ring controlled by the family was the bookmaking operations that collected money for bets on sporting events. Just like the lottery, runners from each betting parlor located in a tavern, bar, barbershop, social club, or any private club carried the cash and betting slips to the Mafia's bank. Customers who picked the winner received their money back, plus a premium of extra cash based on the winning odds established by the bookmaker.

***

O'Keefe was annoyed that they weren't permitted to interview Provenzano, so he and Murphy walked across the street to Carlson's house. He was sitting on his porch smoking a cigarette, watching them approach.

O'Keefe made the introduction. "Hello, Mr. Carlson. We met earlier, and we'd like to ask you some follow-up questions about today's shooting."

Carlson answered, "You bet. Whatever you need."

"The two police officers who arrived first on the scene told us you were in your living room watching television when the shooting started. Can you tell us again what happened?" O'Keefe said.

Carlson said, "I gave the patrolmen a detailed statement, but I'll summarize the key facts."

When he finished, Murphy asked, "Are you certain it was Sal and Joey who were firing the shotguns and not someone else?"

"Of course, I am. I've known Sal for years, ever since his kids were little. Nice guy. That is, to me, anyway."

O'Keefe looked at his notes from his discussions with the two patrolmen and asked some follow-up questions. He ended by saying, "Thank you, Mr. Carlson. Would you be willing to testify at a trial?"

Carlson responded, "Absolutely. Amy's a special little girl. It was heartbreaking to see her shot up like that. I hope and pray she makes it through surgery." He dragged hard on his cigarette; a cylinder of ash dangled from the end.

With the interview complete, O'Keefe and Murphy walked across the street to Mrs. Walker's house. O'Keefe knocked on her door, and she answered after a few moments.

"Hi, Mrs. Walker. This is Detective Murphy, and I'm Detective O'Keefe. We understand you called the station to report that you heard gunshots."

Mrs. Walker said, "Oh, yes. I heard these strange noises outside and went out the front door to find out what was going on. When I stepped out onto the porch, I heard loud bang, bang, bang sounds. It was terrifying.

When I turned toward where they were coming from, I saw flames and smoke shooting out of the front of the Provenzanos' house."

Murphy asked, "Did you see who was firing the weapons?"

Mrs. Walker answered, "No, but the explosions were coming from inside the house. Oh, and something was whizzing through the air. They looked like a bunch of little black gnats."

O'Keefe responded, "Thank you, ma'am. You're very brave. We're glad you're safe. What else did you see or hear?"

Mrs. Walker said, "Well. I heard something like popping or pinging sounds coming from that van over there."

Murphy asked, "What did you do next?"

She paused to think and said, "I went back into the house and called the police station. I'm still very upset."

O'Keefe responded, "Thank you for calling. Before you went back inside, did you see anyone in the street or coming out of the van?"

Mrs. Walker answered, "No, not until Mr. Carlson came out of his house and went over to the Colters'. He's a war hero, you know, a Marine in the war. They're tough cookies, but he's very kind to me. Since my husband passed a few years ago from a heart

Colter's Code

attack, Mr. Carlson has been helping me by fixing things around the house."

After concluding the interviews, the detectives returned to their car. Inside, O'Keefe clicked on the police radio transmitter and said, "This is Detective O'Keefe. I need you to run a license plate for me: New Jersey plate, Bravo, Lima, Romeo, six, nine, three."

He looked back at the side of the van and wrote down the telephone number painted on the side: 201-766-2947.

Back at the station, O'Keefe called the number. A recorded message answered, "The number you called is no longer in service."

Well, that was a dead end, he thought. *I'll call New Jersey Bell Telephone and get some help.* A supervisor told him that the line was disconnected at the request of the former owner, Carlo Ferrante. He gave O'Keefe Ferrante's address and telephone number. On the next call, Ferrante informed O'Keefe that he had sold the van to a guy named Jimmy Harper.

A secretary placed a note on O'Keefe's desk while he was on the phone. The license plate search confirmed Jimmy Harper owned the van.

Next, O'Keefe called Harper and asked him why his van was parked in front of the Colters'.

He answered, "I tried to park at my friend David Farrell's house down the street, but that was the closest spot I could find. David, Carl Brewer, and I went on a fishing trip at the Jersey Shore, and we drank beer all day. We got so drunk we spent the night down there. What bad luck. Now my van is all shot to hell."

With the search warrant in hand, the detectives headed out the next morning to the Provenzanos'. Before they even got out of the police station parking lot, Rosa Esposito, who was on the Genovese payroll and worked as a clerk in the judge's office, telephoned Lautenberg to alert him that a judge had just signed a search warrant for the Provenzano residence. She knew the Mafia rewarded prompt information. Her brown envelope was substantially thicker the next week.

Lautenberg called Sal: "The court just issued the search warrant, and the detectives are on their way. I'll be there in twenty minutes. If they arrive before I do, don't say a word. Is anyone else in the house?"

Sal answered, "Yeah, my wife and daughter."

Lautenberg said, "We don't want them to get all emotional and say something we don't need right now."

"I understand." Sal asked Carla to take Maria over to the Morettis' house for a few hours.

Carla asked if everything was all right, and Sal told her the police were coming but not to worry. He'd handle it.

O'Keefe and Murphy arrived ten minutes before Lautenberg and knocked on the front door.

After they showed Sal the search warrant, Sal invited the detectives into the living room.

Once inside, Sal said, "My attorney, Frank Lautenberg, is joining us. Can I get you guys a cup of coffee while we wait?"

O'Keefe answered, "No thank you; we're good." Then, he noticed the newly replaced front window and freshly cleaned carpet. He looked around the living room. There wasn't one shred of evidence indicating a shooting. *Damn!* he thought. *We waited too long to search this place.*

O'Keefe asked his first question after Lautenberg arrived. "Mr. Provenzano, would you please describe the events before and after the shooting here yesterday?"

Before Sal answered that first question, Lautenberg interrupted, saying, "Detective, please make your questions more specific."

O'Keefe's rephrased his question and the interview continued.

During the course of the interview, Sal admitted, "Yes. I was home yesterday. Yes, I recently replaced the front living room window glass and cleaned the carpet. And yes, I noticed the van parked outside in the street."

But key questions remained unanswered. Questions like: *Did you own or have in your possession shotguns and double-aught ammunition on the day of the shooting? Did you shoot the van? What motivated you to shoot the van parked in the street?*

Lautenberg had replied to each probing question, "My client invokes his Fifth Amendment right to not answer that question under the grounds the answer might incriminate him."

After the unfruitful interview, the detectives and a police photographer searched the house and didn't find a shred of evidence linking Sal or Joey to the shooting.

Chapter 5
The Hunt for John Colter

Philip Castellano was furious because someone had dared to attack his family. He ordered an exhaustive search to find Sal's killer and enlisted an army of thousands of soldiers and associates from the other four New York Mafia families to hunt for the wino. The reward was substantial, especially for wannabe mobsters hoping to gain favor in the organization. Castellano felt confident Tony and Bruno were not in on the hit, but the curious question remained: *Why did the killer leave them alive?* He ordered Angelo to find the answer. He knew Angelo, as a member of the Black Hand, had acquired special skills to ferret out the truth while keeping his victims alive in excruciating pain and suffering.

He didn't understand Angelo's pleasure in torturing people. But Castellano knew his underboss always extracted the motives and truth to answer every question. Angelo had evolved into a sociopath over many years, starting during his abusive childhood. The triggering event had been in high school, when his alcoholic father came home drunk from the bar one night and went into one of his tirades. He had begun yelling and screaming at Angelo and threatened to beat him black and blue. But Angelo wasn't a little boy anymore, and in an uncontrolled outburst, he violently beat his father to death with a baseball bat.

A few years after killing his father, Angelo made his bones in the Genovese crime family by shooting a store owner who refused to make his extortion payments. Angelo nonchalantly walked into his store and asked the owner how he was doing that day. The owner answered in a friendly manner, and Angelo pulled out a Colt .38 Snub Nose Special and shot him twice in the chest.

Each of his subsequent murders had calloused his heart. He was no longer human. He was one of Lucifer's angels incarnate.

At Castellano's direction, Angelo drove Bruno and Tony to a secluded warehouse on Marsh Street near the Port Newark Channel. There, the screams of his victims would fade away in the wind blowing over the Meadowlands.

Bruno was the first to have his arms and legs duct-taped to a chair. Angelo knew the fear of witnessing the physical torture of another human created an effective image for the next interrogation, so Tony was held by two soldiers and forced to watch. Angelo lumbered to the workbench and selected a black electric drill to begin the questioning.

The sight of the large drill bit sent panic through the minds of Bruno and Tony as they imagined the pain in their bodies from the spinning steel deeply penetrating their soft flesh. They had once been witnesses to Angelo's torture treatments.

Angelo stood over Bruno. The drill bit entered Bruno's right knee, tearing through the flesh and soliciting agonized screams. The loud buzzing noise of the electric motor added to the horror. Tony watched in terror as Bruno's blood and flesh dripped off the steel tip onto the cement floor.

Angelo asked, "Who killed Sal, and why did you help them?"

Bruno shouted, "I don't know. I didn't help anybody."

"Then why didn't the killer shoot you and Tony?" Angelo demanded.

Bruno begged, "I don't know. Please stop!"

Angelo drilled a hole in Bruno's left kneecap and shouted, "I asked you who killed Sal. Tell me the truth and I'll stop. If you don't, there's plenty of body parts left to drill: your elbows, hips, and what about …" Bruno shrieked as Angelo hovered the drill between his legs.

Bruno almost passed out watching red liquid oozing out of his throbbing knees as he anticipated the drill bit continuing its journey.

He whimpered, "Angelo, I told you, I don't know. I didn't have anything to do with it." He started crying in complete submission, not knowing how to make the drilling stop.

The spinning steel found new flesh to explore. Bruno screamed and screamed until relief arrived when his body slumped over, bound to the chair.

Angelo paced slowly toward Tony. "Tell me: why did you betray Sal?"

Aghast, watching the drill come closer, he pleaded, "Look, Angelo. You've known me for years. I attended your daughter's birthday party and your son's baptism. Please. Please. We weren't helping anyone. We were trying to protect Sal. Then that bomb thing went off. I told you before, we ran after the guy to catch him." Dejected, he added, "But we just couldn't find him."

The spinning bit penetrated Tony's hip socket, splattering blood and white bone across Angelo's pant leg.

"You're lying to me. Tell me the truth," Angelo snarled.

Crying in despair, Tony made his last attempt at salvation. "I am telling you the truth. I didn't have anything to do with it."

Bruno and Tony died innocent soldiers, unable to identify the wino assassin. Their tortured body parts were never found, dumped with a routine load of garbage from a barge in the Ambrose Channel off the coast of Sandy Hook, New Jersey.

Angelo liked Bruno and Tony but felt no remorse about inflicting pain, watching them suffer, and then ending their lives. He thought to himself, *I'll catch this wino guy. It's just a matter of time before he hears this spinning drill.*

What Angelo didn't know was the wino had escaped using countermeasures of deception to conceal his true identity. Before John made the final decision to start a war with the Genovese crime syndicate, he had devised an intricate plan using disguises and escape routes to vanish without leaving a trace. He knew the coal-mining strip pits around Pittsburg, Kansas, entombed more dead bodies than the Meadowlands in New Jersey. He didn't want to join them as a permanent resident.

***

After John safely returned to Kansas, he decided to mentally reexamine each phase of his plan. He needed to know if he had made a mistake that would jeopardize his family. He started by retracing each step, starting with establishing his alibi. *I drove from Pittsburg on the interstate southeast to the Appalachian Trailhead in Georgia. That's the opposite direction of New York City.*

When I arrived at the trailhead, I discovered a remote private parking lot on a nearby farm that charged a daily fee. They recorded my license plate number and the dates I was there.

From there, I hiked twenty miles north into the wilderness. No one on the trail would remember just another hiker traveling the trail wearing sunglasses and a hat. I sure enjoyed waking up to the sound of the wind blowing through the treetops and the birds singing a morning serenade. Watching the orange sunrise over the mountaintop was a special treat. Every time I connect with nature like that, it's a memorable experience.

John continued to mentally retrace his journey to New York City. *Let's see. I left the Appalachian Trail and hiked into town, where I boarded the next train north.* His memory replayed the ride past waves of grain-filled farmlands, picturesque valleys bordered by majestic mountains, sparkling streams, and roaring rivers. He was sad when it changed farther north from beautiful scenic pathways to pictures painted dingy brown as the train meandered through decaying cities such as Baltimore, Philadelphia, and Newark.

When he was finished recalling the first leg of his journey, he confidently concluded, *There's no way anyone could discover my path from Kansas to New York.*

He continued his thought process. *When I arrived in New York, I stayed at an old family friend's house. The Browns held me at the hospital the day I was born. They watched whimsical ocean waves lick my tiny toes at the beach while I sat in diapers by the Atlantic Ocean's edge, gleefully eating green seaweed.* He thought to himself, *No one will connect me to the Browns.*

At Sparks Restaurant, I cloaked my stocky six-two frame in a thick coat and hunched over, dressed as a wino. That flash-bang grenade worked perfectly. Those guys were completely shocked. Even if they found my disguise in the garbage bag in that dumpster, there'd be no way to trace it back to me.

When I went into the subway, I kept looking back before I boarded the train. No one followed me. And in Lower Manhattan, I changed directions several times before getting on the ferry. He smiled. *I disappeared into the city like the morning mist evaporating as the sun rises above the horizon. I thought it was a nice touch depositing the murder weapon in a brown paper bag at the bottom of the Hudson River Bay.*

***

Back at Genovese headquarters, a voice cried out, "Hey, Angelo, there's a guy on the phone for you named Al Jones with the Newark Police Department, and he says he has information about those grenades."

Angelo answered gruffly, "This is Angelo."

"Hello, Mr. Galante. I did some checking around and found out there are two stores in the New York area that sell explosive devices like the one you described. One is Big John's Gun Shop over in Secaucus, New Jersey, and the other is the Jamaica

Sporting Goods store in Brooklyn. I also checked with some contacts in the NYPD. They said their SWAT team uses flash-bang grenades, but stuff like that is secured in restricted-access lockers. None are unaccounted for. Same thing here in Newark. No one has requisitioned any grenades in the last six months. They're kept under strict controls. You want me to check out those gun shops for you?"

Angelo replied, "No. We'll do that. Thanks for your help."

Angelo shared the good news with Philip Castellano, confident they would soon identify Sal's killer.

They finally had the lead they needed. Angelo thought to himself, *This wino guy will soon be mine. Then I'll kill him and his whole family.* He enjoyed hunting his prey, but the kill was ecstasy.

Castellano ordered Angelo to pick his best soldiers and go to Brooklyn. Angelo noted the location of the Jamaica Sporting Goods store then said, "Boss. That's Vito Bonanno's turf. You want me to call him first?"

He answered, "No. I'll take care of that. You just get over there and see what you can find."

Castellano made the call. "This is Castellano. I need to speak to Vito."

A man answered, "Godfather. Vito's out right now. I'll have him call you as soon as he gets here."

Minutes later, the telephone rang. It was Vito. Castellano explained he needed permission to interrogate a businessman in his territory and why.

Vito answered, "Yes, godfather. Whatever you need."

Angelo and his men walked into the Jamaica Sporting Goods store and asked the clerk if the owner was in.

The clerk answered lazily, "Yeah, I'll get him for you."

An older man entered and said, "Hi. I'm Jerry Reynolds. What can I do for you gentlemen?"

Angelo said, "A friend of ours, Vito, sent us over. I am looking for something special called a flash-bang grenade. You got any?"

Jerry about wet his pants when Angelo said Vito had sent him. Jerry religiously made his Bonanno extortion payments without hesitation. Jerry's mouth became so dry with fear, he was almost unable to speak. He muttered, "Yes." And without thinking about the consequences, he instinctively added, "We sell those, but you need a special license. I'll have to write your name, address, and license number in the ledger book. The ATF requires me to keep a list of anyone who buys them."

Angelo curtly responded, "You don't need that. Give me the goddamn list."

Mark E. Uhler

Jerry realized he had made a bad mistake and hoped he wouldn't be severely punished. The men standing before him looked like they were charter members of Murder, Inc. He handed Angelo the list.

The list contained several purchases but only one sale in the last six months. Gary Rogers, 1453 West Union Blvd., Islip, New York. He had purchased a box of six.

"What can you tell me about this Rogers guy?" Angelo demanded.

Jerry started to tremble and said, "Well, all I know is what he told me. He owns a security company on Long Island and was in the Special Forces in Vietnam. Now he helps rich clients in the Hamptons and Montauk." Angelo tore the page out of the ledger and walked out.

Later, Angelo telephoned Captain O'Malley with the New York Police Department. O'Malley answered and Angelo said, "This is Angelo. You know anything about a guy named Rogers who runs a private security company in Islip?"

O'Malley answered, "Not much, but I've heard about the guy. He's a real badass. Rumor has it that in Vietnam he liked to kill the gooks up close and personal using a Recon Bowie knife. Give me a few minutes to make some calls."

Angelo waited.

"Here's what I found out," O'Malley said with a hint of excitement when he called back. "Rogers's military records showed extensive training in tactical combat situations. He had three tours in Vietnam. He's an expert marksman with a pistol and received elite training on how to kill using stealth or extreme force. Two months ago, he rescued some millionaire's daughter out in Montauk using a flash-bang grenade. During the incident, Rogers shot the two kidnappers twice in the chest, then once right between the eyes." He went on to add details about the Rogers family.

The revelation caused Angelo to think of similarities to Sal's hit. *This Rogers guy must be the wino assassin. He has the skills and experience. Sal was shot the same way. Is Rogers a paid hitman working alone to fulfill a contract, or was there another reason he killed Sal?*

Angelo arrived at Rogers's house that evening accompanied by two ruthless enforcers for added firepower armed with automatic .45 Colt pistols. They approached the front door; Angelo gripped a Smith & Wesson Model 19 revolver under his coat. He knocked, but there was no answer. Another knock, this time harder. A faint voice responded, "All right, all right. I'm coming." The porch light came on.

Rogers was working on his fourth two-finger pour of Maker's Mark on the rocks as part of his daily routine to relax after dinner. He had lived alone since the divorce two years earlier. Returning from Vietnam had left him unable to leave the demons back in the jungle.

Opening the front door with highball in hand, Rogers quizzically asked, "Can I help you, buddy?"

Angelo pointed the Smith & Wesson at Rogers's face while the two soldiers stepped into view. Rogers considered knocking the gun out of Angelo's hand—he knew he could by using his combat training—but the whiskey combined with two other men pointing guns at his head convinced him the effort would be in vain.

"Let's go inside. We want to ask you some questions," Angelo snapped. Then he threatened, "We know where your ex-wife Kathy and son William live. Cooperate and they won't be harmed. Turn around and put your hands behind your back."

"What's this all about? What do you guys want?" Rogers asked, now getting irritated. Before turning, he reasoned, *Should I do what this guy wants? Once he ties my hands, I have no chance to fight back. I could kill at least the guy with the Smith & Wesson with one blow to the throat and crush his larynx. Maybe even another one of these guys, but then I'm dead.* He turned around in submission.

"Sit over there on the couch," Angelo ordered after they tied his wrists. Angelo pointed to one soldier and said, "Go search the house." He dragged a chair across the room, setting it about three feet in front of Rogers. The other soldier stood pointing his Colt at Rogers's chest.

Angelo barked, "You bought some flash-bang grenades at the Jamaica Sporting Goods store in Brooklyn. What did you do with them?"

"I used a couple of them for a job. The rest are downstairs in the basement with all my gear," Rogers replied. "Some of my clients and their children from time to time need extraction from difficult situations, such as kidnapping. When involving the police is not an option, they hire me to bring the family member home safely. I use the grenades to stun the perps, and then I restrain them. Once neutralized, I turn them over to the authorities."

"Show me," Angelo commanded.

At the foot of the stairs, Rogers announced, "They're over there in that box. That one on the workbench."

Angelo glared at the assortment of handguns, rifles, shotguns, and ammunition scattered everywhere. The room resembled an armory. He opened the box and found the grenades, goggles, and ear plugs. Holding up the goggles and ear plugs he asked, "What are these for?"

Rogers replied, "You wear ear plugs to stop the explosion's shock wave from stunning you. If you don't wear them, you'll be temporarily disoriented. The goggles block the flash so you're not blinded."

"How many did you buy?" Angelo asked.

"I bought six and used two for a job. Let me think for a minute." Rogers then said, "I used one for training to simulate a takedown to prepare for the job and stay sharp. I used another during the job to extract a hostage."

Angelo's tone and questions intensified. Rogers's answers were not what Angelo wanted to hear. Angelo decided his special skills were needed to glean the truth. The screams echoed from the concrete walls.

Rogers answered his captor's questions under extreme duress: "No, I've never heard of Sal Provenzano. No, I'm not a hitman. No, I didn't give any grenades to anyone. And no. I didn't kill this Sal guy." An hour later, as excruciating pain ravaged his body, Rogers regretted not trying to kill the three intruders at the front door. He welcomed death to stop the pain. His mutilated body was never found.

The next morning, Angelo and his henchmen went to Big John's Gun Shop over in Secaucus, New Jersey. The questioning resulted in another dead end. The store did sell flash-bang grenades, but their records indicated the last sale was over a year ago.

The hunt for Sal's killer turned from anticipation to frustration. Angelo was perplexed. He had no clue

Colter's Code

who the wino assassin was. *Where did he come from? And why did he kill Sal?*

He decided to take a closer look at the rival Newark gang, The Family, controlled by Willie Jefferson. Angelo didn't think he had the guts to make such a bold attack, but Willie had strong motives, including money, prestige, and power. He thought, *Maybe Jefferson launched an assault on Sal's territory to expand his cocaine and marijuana distribution. But would he risk all-out war? Hell, he only had about two hundred men. Combined with the other four families, we have thousands of soldiers. And that's just in New York. Castellano rules the commission and has access to thousands more from all across the country.*

He continued his reasoning: *Sure, we may kill a few soldiers now and again in turf battles but killing a high-level capo? That's suicide.* The cost of retribution outweighed the perceived benefits, and that principle had governed the streets for years.

Angelo knew how to find the answer. He ordered his soldiers to kidnap two of The Family's crew members and meet him at Tuffy's Butcher Shop in Newark. The interrogation began with one man tied to a chair in the cutting room while the other was sequestered in the refrigerated meat locker. Inside, he was hung by his hands like a dressed carcass of prime beef.

Forcefully, Angelo started the inquisition: "My name is Angelo. I'm going to ask you some questions and you will answer them to my satisfaction without hesitation. You play games with me, and your body will suffer more pain than you could ever imagine possible." He paused as the man's level of fear rose like mercury in a thermometer on a hot summer day. "Tell me what you know about the killing of Sal Provenzano."

With a tough-guy attitude, the first victim answered, "We don't know nothin', man. Who the hell is he?"

"Wrong answer!"

Angelo ordered one of his men to untie the belligerent's left arm and hold it firmly on the meat cutting table. Then, Angelo grabbed a meat tenderizing mallet. The coarse side shaped like pyramids smashed the man's left thumb and index finger. His body jolted and he screamed.

Angelo demanded, "I asked you what you know about the killing of Sal Provenzano. Sal was a capo in our organization."

"I told you, motherfucker, we don't know nothin' 'bout that."

Angelo raised the blood-stained mallet to strike the man's other fingers.

He shouted in terror, "Look, man, we may get orders to kill some low-level guys over a street corner or two, but no one in our crew had orders to kill this guy Sal. Nobody's crazy enough to kill a capo." The pain and suffering intensified.

Angelo ordered one of his soldiers to bring in the second man. As he entered the room, he clearly read the visual message from the sight of his partner's tortured and mutilated body.

Angelo repeated the process. "You lie, you suffer." Under questioning, the second man admitted he had heard of Sal Provenzano but had no idea who killed him.

Angelo pointed to the first sacrifice and said to one of his soldiers, "Kill him."

A bullet exploded into the man's temple, splattering blood and pieces of white brain matter all over the second guy's face. Blood crawled down his cheek. He wailed uncontrollably.

Angelo shouted, "Tell me who killed Sal Provenzano or you're next. I'll kill every last one of your crew if I have to."

The Genovese soldier pressed the handgun against the man's forehead. The five remaining large-caliber copper-tipped bullets were staring at him from their silver-colored cylinders, waiting to end his life.

He yelled, "I told you, man! We didn't have anything to do with that."

Their bodies disappeared in the Meadowlands. The crabs enjoyed their feast for several days.

Angelo was satisfied Jefferson's crew had not participated in the hit on Sal. It was time to look outside of the usual suspects and motives involving rival Mafia families or warring gangs. He had a new idea to expand the hunt for the wino and dialed Detective Miller.

"This is Angelo," he said. "Can you think of anyone in the Colter family who would kill Sal?"

Miller paused, scrolling through names in his memory circuits, then said, "Amy's father died a hero in Vietnam. Her mother, Linda, has a sister named Donna. They certainly had a strong motive, but neither one is capable of killing Sal. The only one I can think of is John Colter. He's her uncle. You might have seen him at Sal and Joey's trial. He's the big guy who sat behind the table for the prosecution. The uncle certainly had motive."

"Tell me more about this uncle. Where does he live?"

Miller answered, "The guy lives way out in the sticks in a little town called Pittsburg, Kansas, somewhere south of Kansas City, Missouri. He owns a manufacturing company and is really rich. Apparently, he retired from running the company and became a college professor. I think he teaches economics, but—"

Angelo interrupted, "If he's so rich, why the hell is he teaching at some university in hillbilly country?"

Miller said, "I don't know. But I do know he invented an electrical device that is sewn into bathing suits and repels sharks. It's sold all over the world. I know from personal experience it really works. Two summers ago, a shark was swimming right at me, but as soon as it sensed the electrical field emitted from the thing, it turned away. Turns out the guy grew up in Maplewood, New Jersey, and went to college out in Kansas years ago. He liked it so much, he stayed. His wife grew up out there and they have two kids."

Angelo wanted to know more and said, "Do some checking, and find out if he was out here when Sal was killed."

Miller replied, "You got it. Let me do some digging around and get back to you."

A few days later, Miller called Angelo. "I got some more information on that uncle, John Colter. His Kansas driver's license lists him at six foot two with blue eyes, and he weighs 240 pounds. Immediate family members include his wife, Debbie, a son named Jack, and a daughter named Lori. No criminal record of any kind."

Angelo responded, "This uncle's a pretty big guy. Does he have any military background?"

Miller answered, "No. Only his deceased brother."

Angelo thought, *Maybe I need to visit Pittsburg. I'll find out if this guy was the wino assassin.*

Miller continued, "I checked Colter's credit card records and searched for any charges in the New York area during the time of Sal's shooting. I found purchases for plane tickets and the usual stuff during the time periods around the funeral, trial, and one other visit to New Jersey, but nothing since then. I did find a gas charge at a Mobil gas station in Paducah, Kentucky, three days before Sal was killed and one at an Exxon station in Chattanooga, Tennessee, the day after Sal was killed. He bought some camping supplies at a store in the Amicalola Falls State Park in Georgia. I called the store and asked about the purchase. A young store clerk named Bonnie answered and said the park is really popular with hikers because it's the southern end of the Appalachian Trail. I asked how far it was from New York and she said about nine hundred miles. That's just one way. It would take months to hike up here and back."

Angelo pondered, *The hiking story sounds plausible, but this guy Colter had a powerful motive.*

He decided to call his old friend Joseph DeLuna, the underboss of the Civella crime family in Kansas City, before making a trip way out to Pittsburg himself.

"Joe, this is Angelo. I need your help checking out a guy in your territory."

Joe said, "Sure. Anything you need. It's yours. Who's the guy and where's he from?"

Colter's Code

What DeLuna and Galante didn't realize was the FBI had placed wiretaps on DeLuna's phone as part of an ongoing investigation into the connection between the Teamsters Union pension funds and the Tropicana Hotel in Las Vegas. The FBI had learned that the Civella crime family members skimmed cash off the top of casino profits and then boarded TWA flights with suitcases full of cash for delivery to Civella in Kansas City. The cash was subsequently shared with Mafia families in Chicago, Detroit, and New York.

Angelo answered, "The guy's name is John Colter. He lives in some small town called Pittsburg."

Joe responded, "Yeah, I know Pittsburg well. We have strong friends down there, especially in Frontenac. No telling how many bodies we disappeared in the strip pits around Pittsburg. During Prohibition, the family made a lot of booze down there. The whole Crawford County Sheriff's Department and all the judges were on our payroll. We still go bird hunting down there with Nicholas Aiuppa, the boss in Chicago. He loves Gebhardt's fried chicken, coleslaw, and German potato salad." Joe laughed. "One time, he shot so many birds down there his whole trunk was full of quail. Game warden caught him up by the Holiday Inn."

The FBI agents on the phone listened inquisitively. Who was John Colter, and why was he so important that the New York Mafia was asking about him?

The call ended with Joe's pledge to personally make the inquiries into Colter. He started making phone calls to various sources in the Pittsburg area. He learned that John had graduated from Pittsburg State University with degrees in accounting and economics. In college, he had invented an underwater electrical device that prevented shark attacks and subsequently founded a manufacturing company in Pittsburg. The company shipped the device all over the United States using Frontenac Trucking Company, which was owned by Civella. So, DeLuna called the head of the Teamsters to make some inquires. The loading dock workers at the plant reported that John had recently been out of town.

DeLuna uncovered from another associate that the local Pittsburg *Morning Sun Newspaper* had published a series of stories about John's hiking trips all over the country as part of an ongoing adventure series. The articles detailed John's expeditions into perilous environments such as the deadly depths of the Grand Canyon, the remote, punishing desert in Canyonlands, Utah, and the hazardous, high-altitude country of the Sierra Nevada Mountains.

One of the most exciting articles described the attack by a hungry mountain lion while John was hiking in the mountains near Red River, New Mexico. Harsh winter conditions had ravaged the vicious predator's food sources, and it was stalking John for his next meal. Just before the ambush, John had noticed movement in the woods out of the corner of his eye. *What was that*, he wondered. He turned, searched intently, and withdrew his Barretta nine-millimeter pistol. Just then, the cougar leaped into the air to kill its prey. Instinctively, John managed to pull the trigger. The mountain lion was killed instantly, but its momentum knocked John down and it landed right on his chest. Later that night, John walked into the Bull o' the Woods Saloon in Red River covered in blood. He was carrying its head and fur pelt over his shoulder. The patrons went wild.

After DeLuna relayed the new information to Angelo, Angelo started digesting everything he had learned about Uncle John. The pieces of the puzzle slowly formed a mental picture. He had a motive and possessed the skills to do the job. He asked himself, *Does this uncle have the guts to attack one of us? I don't know, but I'm going to find out.*

He reconsidered what Detective Miller told him about John's credit cards. The activity suggested that he was hiking the Appalachian Trail. Was he really? *Maybe I'll just kill him and eliminate any doubt*, he thought.

Angelo called Miller. "I need you to find out more about this Colter guy's hiking trip to Georgia. Find out if it was just his alibi and if he really took a detour to New York City."

Mark E. Uhler

Miller reconsidered the credit card statements and the two purchases for gasoline on the route to Georgia. He pondered, *If John drove his Jeep from Georgia to New York and purchased gasoline with cash, it'd be untraceable.* He had an idea. *Toll booths have cameras. I'll review the camera footage and look for John's Jeep.*

He contacted the New Jersey State Police to obtain copies of the tapes for the nearby Edison Toll Plaza on Interstate 95. It was on the main route from Georgia to New York City. When he received the large volume of tapes, he realized that it was too time-consuming for one person. He called the police academy for manpower. *Problem solved*, he thought to himself. The cadets dutifully watched the tapes hoping to solve the big case for Detective Miller but finished without finding a Jeep matching John's license plate. Miller was disappointed and thought to himself, *I'm not going to give up. Angelo's reward could be life-changing.*

He redialed the camping supply store in Amicalola Falls State Park, hoping to speak to the same clerk.

A man answered with a deep Southern accent. Miller said, "Hi. This is Detective Miller, with the Newark, New Jersey, Police Department. Is Bonnie there?"

The man replied, "Yep, she sure is." He placed his hand over the receiver and yelled, "Hey, Bonnie. You got a phone call from some guy who says he's Detective Miller. Said he talked to you last week."

Miller heard some rustling on the other end, and then someone picked up the phone. "Hi. This is Bonnie," she said in an excited tone.

"Hi, Bonnie. This is Detective Miller again. Thank you for helping me last week. I have a few follow-up questions."

In her deep Georgia drawl, she said, "Absolutely, detective."

Miller asked, "When people hike the Appalachian Trail, where do they park their vehicles?"

"Well, sir, there's parking about a mile from the trailhead, but it's not very safe to leave your car there. There's lots of break-ins. Most people park in a field on the Sutherland Farm. They grow lots of peaches, don't cha know. That delicious freestone kind. The Sutherlands charge a fee and check the cars each day to make sure no one's broken in and stolen anything. I doubt if anyone would even try. Mr. Sutherland is a mean cuss. He'll shoot your ass if he catches you inside the big metal fence messin' with one of those cars. Oh. And at night, their dog, Big Brutus, guards the property. That rottweiler is a vicious one. He'd bite your leg off."

Miller responded, "That's very helpful. Thank you."

Bonnie replied cheerfully, "Anything to help the po-lice! You ever get down here, you be sure to get some of those Sutherland peaches."

Miller called the operator in Dawsonville, Georgia, to obtain the telephone number of the Sutherlands.

A young boy dressed in blue Wrangler coveralls and muddy cowboy boots answered, "Hello? Sutherland residence, who may I say is calling?"

"Hi. This is Detective Miller calling from the Newark, New Jersey, Police Department. Is Mr. Sutherland there?"

The boy hollered, "Hey, Daddy. You got a phone call! It must be important. He said he's a police detective."

Leroy Sutherland hurried in from the living room wondering, *What in the world would a police detective want with me?* "Thank you, son," he said. Junior handed him the black receiver attached by wire to the wooden wall Western Electric. Leroy leaned into the black mouthpiece and answered in an inquisitive voice, "This is Mr. Sutherland. May I help you?"

Miller said, "Yes, I hope so. I'm Detective Miller with the Newark, New Jersey, Police Department. We are trying to locate a missing person for some relatives up here. Their nephew from Kansas drove out there to Georgia to hike the Appalachian Trail a while back, and the family hasn't heard from him since he left. It was his mother's birthday last week and he always calls her to wish her happy birthday. He never called and they got concerned, so they called me. I'm an old family friend and they asked me to make some inquiries to find out if he's OK. I understand some hikers park their vehicles at your farm while they hike the Appalachian Trail. Do you keep any records of who parked there?"

Leroy answered, "Yes, sir. We charge a daily, weekly, or monthly fee and write down every name. Next to it we add the license plate number, the day they arrive, and the day they leave."

Miller asked, "Could you check a name and license plate number for me and tell me when the car was there?"

He responded, "Sure, detective. What's the name and number?"

"John Colter. Crawford County, Kansas license, A as in alpha, L as in lima, B as in bravo, six, six, one." He added the dates of interest.

"I'll check. Let me look at the record book." The black earpiece dangled from the wire while Miller patiently waited.

Leroy grabbed the ledger from his brown rolltop desk and started reading. *Let's see, where are those dates? Oh, here, I found them.* He went back and said, "Detective Miller. I found those dates you gave me.

Yep. John Colter's Jeep was parked here that whole time."

After Miller thanked Leroy and hung up the phone, the wheels in his detective mind started turning. The dates showed the Jeep had been parked at the farm during the time gap between gas station stops. So, John hadn't driven his Jeep to New York City. How else could he have gotten there? He had an epiphany: maybe he had taken a train.

Miller knew the security cameras at the train station filmed every passenger arriving on Amtrak trains originating from Union Station in Washington, DC. *All I have to do is look at train maps showing routes from Georgia to Union Station. Once I find the connection, I can search the train schedule tables for plausible times. Then, I've got my starting point. After that, all I need is those tapes.*

The New York City Police Department delivered copies of the film the next day after Miller told them Angelo Galante demanded their immediate cooperation.

Miller sat beside the technician at the police crime lab, and they methodically searched the films for a picture of John. The blurry-eyed pair gave up eight hours later.

"Damn. No one matched. Another dead end," he said to the tech.

Miller didn't realize how successfully John's disguise had altered his appearance. Even if one of his students had been standing next to him, they wouldn't have recognized him as their professor. They would have just been looking at another gray-bearded old man.

Miller called Angelo and gave him the disappointing report.

"Everything checked out. Looks like John was hiking in Georgia. I confirmed with the locals that his Jeep was parked there the whole time. Then I wondered if he took a train, so I reviewed the film from the station's security cameras. No John. I even checked bus schedules and found that with all the stops in every little town from the Port Authority Bus Terminal to Georgia, it was impossible to make a round trip in the time frame he was gone. I also asked some of my airport contacts to check the passenger lists on flights from Georgia to New York. There's no record of a John Colter."

Chapter 6
The Hospital Trauma Center

The hospital intercom system announced the request for the immediate mobilization of the senior surgery team in the trauma center. Van Buren silenced the screaming sirens. The emergency entryway doors opened to accept the next life battling the pain and suffering of human existence.

Linda escorted the gurney into the emergency room and watched fearfully as the nurses slid Amy's fragile body onto the examination table. There, they gently rolled her to one side and removed the orange board from underneath her back. The resident on duty inserted an intubation tube and attached it to a respirator to force air into Amy's lungs. Surgeon Dr. David Schaeffer, already dressed in scrubs, rushed into the room and started his examination of the traumatic gunshot wounds. He was surprised the little girl was still alive.

Linda stood by watching helplessly. Her husband, Jack, was resting in the white stone fields of Arlington Cemetery. The hooded gray ghost called the Grim Reaper laid his scythe down in the emergency room to take Amy to meet her father.

After his initial examine, Dr. Schaeffer ordered the medical team to move the patient to the operating room. He knew from his experience as a MASH surgeon in Vietnam time was running out. The survival rate for gunshot casualties with head wounds like Amy's was marginal at best. The three bullet holes in her chest reduced her chances even further.

Linda began to cry as they rolled Amy into the operating room. The doors closed behind her. The hooded ghost followed.

The X-ray technician secured the black-and-white images onto the illuminated screen. Dr. Schaeffer traced the entry point of the three pellets through the lungs to the exit holes in Amy's back. That's when he noticed the dark shadows in her chest. He knew fluids were filling her lungs and her life was sliding into the abyss of terminal darkness. The anesthesiologist announced Amy's pulse and blood pressure were approaching critically low levels.

Dr. Schaeffer looked down at the resilient little girl fighting to stay alive and with resolve announced, "All right, people. We're going to save this little girl. Do your job well. Be her savior today. First, we're going to drain that fluid in her lungs. Scalpel, please."

Linda anxiously sat alone in the visitors waiting room watching the hands on the wall clock tick at a snail's pace as the doctors and nurses skillfully battled the Grim Reaper as he tugged at Amy's soul.

She silently cried out in desperation, *Oh God. Please save my little Amy. She's all I have. Be merciful and send your angels to heal her broken body.* Suddenly, she was overwhelmed by a peace that passed all understanding.

Late that afternoon, over twelve hundred miles away, John answered the telephone to hear his secretary, Kathy, announce a call on line two from a man named Andy Morgan. She added that he said he was an old high school friend living back in Maplewood, New Jersey. John wondered why he was calling.

He answered with excitement, "Andy, how are you? It's been a long time."

How am I going to tell John about the shooting? Andy thought. He answered, "Yes, it has, John. You remember I work for the Maplewood Police Department, right?"

"Yes, of course I do. You always wanted to do good and help other people. How's life in Maplewood?"

Andy changed from a friendly tone to a concerned voice. "Well, that's why I called. I am afraid I have some bad news." He paused to swallow. "And as your friend I wanted to tell you before anyone else called you."

Listening intently, John's mood changed from happy to apprehensive. He stared out the window toward New Jersey and braced himself for what Andy was about to say next.

Andy continued, "I just talked to two patrol officers who responded to a call in Linda's neighborhood. Two mob guys living in the house across from hers opened fire with high-powered shotguns at a van parked in the street. Some of the pellets missed the van and hit Linda's house. She's OK, but Amy suffered severe injuries—"

Alarmed, John interjected, "Do you know what her condition is?"

"The paramedics arrived at the house and performed triage, then drove Amy to College Hospital in Newark. She's in critical condition with three bullet holes in her chest," he said gravely, then the line went silent as Andy paused to take a deep breath. "John, another pellet hit Amy in the head. She's in surgery right now." He tried to comfort John and said, "I called one of our detectives at the hospital to get more information. He said the doctor performing the operation was one of the best trauma surgeons in the New York area."

John's heart wrenched with the news of Amy's shooting. His emotional cycle changed from disbelief to anger. The Adam's apple in his throat tightened, and his eyes watered as he tried to speak.

He paused to gain his composure and said, "Andy, I appreciate you calling me." He gathered his thoughts and asked, "You said two guys from across the street fired shotguns into Linda's house?"

Andy answered, "Yeah. The neighbor across the street, Sal Provenzano. He's a high-ranking member of a Mafia crime family in New York, but he lives in

Maplewood. Apparently, Sal thought rival gang members were waiting in the van to ambush him when he left the house. He and his son, Joey, decided to eliminate the threat and shoot up the van. Your niece was collateral damage, and her dog was too. The patrolmen at the scene found Max's body on the floor."

John's mind flashed back to the day he had brought Amy the furry, white Labrador puppy. She had smiled from ear to ear with joy. After Jack died, the puppy, whom she had named Max, had helped with the healing process.

Andy added, "John, I am so sorry. Is there anything I can do?"

John replied, "Yes. Andy. What was the name of the hospital again where Amy is in surgery?"

"College Hospital in Newark. It's over on Bergen Street, about five miles from Newark Airport," Andy said.

John asked, "Do you have a phone number?"

"Hold on while I look up the number for you," Andy answered. John heard some rustling of paper and Andy mumbling. "Where's that number? Here it is." Andy picked up the phone. "OK, it's 201-972-4300."

John thanked Andy for the call and telephone number, then ended by asking if he could call Andy later for more details about Sal. Images flashed across John's mind like the frames in a 1920s silent black-

and-white motion picture. Fond memories of watching his brother hold Amy for the first time when she was born, and the first time she called him Uncle John.

After Jack's death, John and Amy had developed a special bond. He had made the extra effort to spend special time with her during family vacations. His memories turned to the Rockefeller Center ice skating rink in New York City, where he had taught Amy how to ice skate. He remembered how she would fall and get right back up time and time again until she circled the rink without falling. He had melted on the ice when she thanked him with a big, excited hug, adding, "I love you, Uncle John."

He took a deep breath and let it out slowly to calm the emotional anger swelling in his body, then called the hospital. A nurse told John that Amy was still in surgery.

John asked his secretary to check airline flights from Kansas City to Newark. Then he dialed his boss, Brett Johnson, the Chairman of the Economics Department at Pittsburg State University. In a melancholy voice, he asked if he could come to his office to discuss an urgent personal matter.

Brett recognized the sadness in John's voice and asked, "Is everything all right?"

John responded, "No, not really. I just got off the phone with an old high school basketball buddy who works for the Maplewood Police Department. There was a shooting in my sister-in-law Linda's neighborhood, and some of the bullets went through her house. She wasn't hurt, but my niece Amy was hit and is in critical condition. She's in surgery right now."

"That's terrible. What can I do to help?" Brett replied.

John said, "I'm going home to tell Debbie and the kids. Then I need some time off to travel to New Jersey. I don't know how long we'll be gone."

Brett responded with empathy, "John, you take as much time as you need. We'll take care of everything here. You go! Be with your family. My wife and I will pray for Amy to recover and for Linda to receive a comforting spirit."

The Colter house was engulfed in a somber mood when John told his family Amy was badly hurt in an accident. He explained they were leaving for the Kansas City Airport to fly to Newark and visit her in the hospital. As John was driving his family northward on US Highway 69, he decided their minds needed a distraction from the sad silence. He asked himself, *What stories can I tell to distract everybody and lighten the mood?* Then he noticed a herd of longhorn cattle grazing in a field of bright-green fescue grass. The peaceful scene reminded him of happy memories while working on a two thousand-acre cattle ranch near Elk City, Kansas, to earn money to help pay college expenses.

I know. I'll tell some random stories about daily life working on the farm, he said to himself, and recounted story after story for the next hour.

The family's favorite story was about when John delivered a baby calf one stormy winter day. Snow had been fiercely falling on the open range, and the north wind was howling. John had been inspecting the herd of cattle when he found a mother cow in deep distress. She was unable to give birth to her calf. So, to save their lives, he had tied the mother's head to a fence post with a rope. Then, he attached a hand winch to a pickup and tied the winch's other end around the calf's hooves trapped inside the mother. He slowly cranked the handle and gently pulled the baby calf out of the birth canal. The next spring, he smiled at the sight of the mother feeding her newborn calf.

Back at the hospital, Detective O'Keefe entered the waiting room to ask Linda questions about the shooting and realized she was still in shock. Her conscious thought was overwhelmed by anxiety caused by the unknown outcome of her daughter's surgery. In a calm, comforting voice, O'Keefe said, "Ms. Colter, I am Detective O'Keefe. I know you're in a lot of pain right now, but I would like to ask you some questions about what happened today." He did not want to upset Linda any further but thought he would try to gain critical details while they were fresh in her mind.

Her sister Donna had arrived moments earlier and looked at the detective with dagger eyes. She said, "Can't this wait? Can't you see she's not capable of answering your questions right now?"

Linda glanced at O'Keefe and answered, "Go ahead. I know it's your job, and you're just trying to help."

O'Keefe said, "Thank you. May I call you Linda?"

She replied, "That would be fine."

O'Keefe added, "I know it's hard to concentrate right now, but please describe as best you can what happened today at your house."

Linda began describing the events in the kitchen and abruptly stopped when she got to the part about entering Amy's room. She said, "That's the last thing I remember." The rest was obscured by a thick fog.

Chapter 7
The Recovery

Dr. Schaeffer walked into the trauma center waiting room, approached Linda, and said, "Linda, your daughter's out of surgery and recovering in the intensive care unit. Amy is a remarkable little girl and a real trooper. She remains in critical condition, but we're encouraged by the outcome of the surgery. Right now, she is sleeping from the sedatives. Let me take you to her room."

Late that evening, the Kansas Colters arrived at the hospital. Jack and Lori joined Donna in the waiting room while John and Debbie walked down the hall to Amy's room. John paused outside the door to take a deep breath and clear his blurry eyes. Debbie squeezed his hand as they walked through the door together. Then, John said with a calm, strong voice, "Linda. I am so sorry."

She stood and they embraced. John looked down at Amy. She was sleeping peacefully, covered with a white hospital blanket. He was distressed when he looked at the intravenous tubes in her tiny arms and the plastic tube pumping precious oxygen into her surgically repaired lungs. He stood there, comprehending the reality of the words spoken across the telephone lines.

Entering the hospital resurrected Debbie's memories working as an emergency room nurse at Breckenridge Hospital in Austin. She had treated victims with gunshot wounds more times than she wanted to remember. The experience was heartwarming when the patients recovered but depressing when they didn't survive.

Debbie examined Amy's head bandages and started reading the chart hanging on the end of the bed. Then, in a confident voice, she said to Linda, "The doctors and nurses are doing a great job." She squeezed Linda's hand.

A few hours passed. Dr. Schaeffer entered the room with a nurse to evaluate Amy's progress and said, "Hi. I'm Dr. Schaeffer. You must be Debbie and John Colter. Linda said you were coming in from Kansas. Your being here is a great comfort for Linda and help to Amy."

Dr. Schaeffer performed his visual evaluation while the nurse took Amy's blood pressure and temperature. He grabbed Amy's chart from the end of the bed and made some additional notes. As he read, he noticed her heart rate: her blood oxygen level and blood pressure had improved a little.

John asked the doctor if they could step out into the hallway, and there he said, "What can you tell us about Amy's prognosis?"

Dr. Schaeffer replied, "We repaired the damage to Amy's lungs and closed the head wound. The immediate concern is the extent of damage to her brain. I am optimistic because she survived a difficult surgery. By itself, that is a miracle given the severity of her wounds combined with the loss of blood. The only thing we can do now is let her body keep fighting and healing."

Later, John drove the family to the hotel to rest after the emotionally charged journey.

As he kissed Lori goodnight, she asked, "Daddy, is Cousin Amy going to be OK?"

John answered, "The wonderful doctors and nurses at the hospital bandaged her wounds and are helping her to recover."

Lori replied, "Daddy, tomorrow, can we bring Amy a new stuffed animal to cheer her up? She really likes bears."

John's heart was moved by her compassion, and he said, "That's a great idea. Will you pick one out for her?" Lori agreed with a sweet smile. Debbie stood listening. Her heart, too, was filled with warmth. She held back tears of joy for her caring daughter and tears of distress for a niece struggling to survive evil acts of violence.

After promising Debbie he would call if there was a material change in Amy's condition, John returned to the hospital that night. Back in the intensive care recovery room, John found Linda sitting next to Amy. She was holding Amy's hand, sound asleep from the emotional stress and exhaustion. He pulled up a chair and sat beside her to watch Amy fight for her life. Then his thoughts shifted to an image of Sal Provenzano: *This Sal guy thinks he can shoot up a van with impunity just because he's in the Mafia. He's so arrogant, he thinks he's above the law and can do whatever he wants. Does he think he won't be accountable and punished for his actions?*

John lived by a different code. A righteous code that was founded on honorable principles such as truth, justice, and protecting others against evil people. Jack had lived by that same code and sacrificed his life in Vietnam defending his country in what the president said was a righteous war against an evil Communist empire.

***

The official army report had said Jack died saving his army brothers during an intense battle on Hill 875. The North Vietnamese Army had moved thousands of troops into the Central Highlands of South Vietnam to exterminate all the American soldiers based near the borders of Cambodia and Laos. The enemy had established a heavily defended position on the hill to lure General Westmoreland into battle. He took the bait. Westmoreland believed the hill provided a target-rich opportunity to kill thousands of enemy soldiers. He ordered two brigades of American soldiers to attack. What followed was thirty-three days of carnage and sustained killing on both sides.

Colter's Code

During the battle, Jack's platoon of thirty-nine men received orders to charge to the top. All around the brave thirty-nine, trees exploded, and bullets ripped through the air. The North Vietnamese feverishly defended the hill, entrenched in their protective bunkers and caves. The platoon leader, Terry Beadle, a Second Lieutenant from Springfield, Missouri, lay dead at the base of the hill. He was a casualty during the first attack. On the second advance, ten more young men died and seventeen were severely wounded climbing the muddy, steep, slippery slope. Heavy machine-gun fire, hand grenades, and mortar shells rained down all around them. Second in command, Sergeant First Class Bill Tolbert, lay unconscious.

Sergeant Jack Colter was now in command. He looked at the remnants of the platoon to assess their ability to fight effectively. Suddenly, a grenade exploded three feet away. The radio operator was killed instantly. Ed Soden, Jack's best friend, was shredded with shrapnel. Over the fog of battle, Jack heard a voice ordering the Americans to retreat and regroup. He relayed the retreat order to his men.

Private Soden was unable to walk, and Jack heaved his body over his right shoulder and zigzagged down the embattled hillside. Jack left Soden with a medic and ran back up the hill and carried another wounded brother to safety. Jack died on the fourth return trip.

The next day, General Westmorland ordered the American soldiers to abandon Hill 875. He had decided it was no longer a military objective.

***

The next morning, Dr. Schaeffer returned to examine Amy. He started reading the chart's notes and statistics, then paused and asked the nurse to retake her blood pressure. The results concerned the doctor because they indicated swelling of the brain. If that was the case, it was restricting vital oxygen necessary for her survival. He reexamined the head wounds but didn't notice anything unusual.

Under normal circumstances, he would have performed a verbal neurological examination to diagnose swelling of the brain. He would have asked her questions such as: "Are you having headaches?" "Are you nauseated?" He would also have listened for difficulty in answering questions, checked for vision problems, and tested for the loss of motor skills. The obstacle was that Amy was unconscious and unable to provide the answers to effectively assess her condition.

Linda asked Dr. Schaeffer in an anxious voice if Amy's condition was improving.

He knew Linda was in despair and that she needed hope and comfort. He calmly responded that Amy was a gritty fighter, and her progress was extraordinary. But she wasn't out of the woods yet.

John intuitively recognized the concern in Dr. Schaeffer's body language during the examination but said nothing to Linda. He thought of what it would be like to see his own daughter lying in that bed. He couldn't imagine how Linda felt. He realized it must be mentally paralyzing.

Dr. Schaeffer exited the room and telephoned a friend to discuss Amy's head injury. Dr. Abraham Rabinowitz was the leading neurosurgeon at the Cornell University Hospital Center. He concurred that her vital signs indicated the possibility of swelling around the brain.

Then he said, "Dr. Schaeffer, I'd like to assist you and help develop Amy's treatment plan. May I come over to Newark and perform an examination as an advising physician? My granddaughter is close to Amy's age and what you just told me about the indiscriminate violence that caused her injuries is very disturbing."

Dr. Rabinowitz arrived that afternoon and performed the examination of Amy's head wound. He complimented Dr. Schaeffer on his skill in repairing the cranium and the treatment protocol. After some discussion, they agreed to change Amy's medications, and her condition improved that evening.

The next day, Dr. Schaeffer returned during his morning routine to examine his patient and noticed more improvement. Then, Amy's eyes fluttered, and she softly said, "Mommy, where am I?"

Linda's heart leaped in relief, and she answered, "You're in the hospital, honey." She hugged her daughter and tears streamed down her cheeks. "You were hurt very badly, and some wonderful doctors and nurses put you back together."

"Like Humpty Dumpty?" Amy weakly responded.

Debbie, Jack, Lori, and John joined Linda in a group hug. Debbie and Linda shared tears of joy. John was heartened by seeing his family held in tight embrace. He hoped the worst was over.

Dr. Schaeffer smiled and said, "Good morning, little lady. It's great to see you're awake. We gave you some strong medicines that helped you take a long nap. How do you feel?"

Amy answered, "My head hurts and I feel like I'm going to throw up."

Debbie looked at John and sent a nonverbal message of concern. She knew those were classic symptoms of swelling of the brain.

Dr. Schaeffer said, "Amy, I'm going to remove some bandages and examine your head."

After observation, he asked, "Amy, your head wound is healing nicely. Are you dizzy at all?"

She answered, "No. But my head still hurts."

He held his right index finger up and said, "I'm going to move my finger and I want you to follow it with your eyes." He watched her eyes follow. They looked normal, and he asked, "Do you see my finger move?"

"Yes. I can see OK."

"Let's play the game 'This Little Piggy' with your toes. You tell me if you feel me pull gently on each toe."

"That tickles," she responded. "My mommy plays 'This Little Piggy' with me at our house."

He decided to reexamine her in a few hours and check again for symptoms of swelling of the brain.

When Dr. Schaeffer returned for his nightly rounds, he thought Amy was sleeping. He attempted to wake her, but she was unconscious. Anxiously, he made a few notes on her chart and asked the nurse to go to the pharmacy and retrieve a different medication.

Lying in bed at the hotel early the next morning, John couldn't stop thinking about the two men who had shot Amy. He called an old friend in the Russell Senate Office Building in Washington, DC.

"Senator Turner's Office. Who may I say is calling?" was the answer.

"This is John Colter. Is the senator in?" he asked.

She straightened up like a soldier coming to attention and said, "Yes, sir. I'll put you right through."

"John. How the hell are you?" the senator hollered.

"Not so good, I'm afraid." He proceeded to describe where he was and why he was there.

"John. I'm so sorry. Your niece Amy is a sweet little girl. Is there anything I can do?"

"Actually, that's why I called. Can you use your contacts to find out what you can about those two Mafia guys I mentioned?"

"Certainly, I'll start by calling Director Kelley at the FBI. Then I'll call Colby over at the CIA. I have lots of friends in this town."

John sighed into the receiver, "Roscoe I really appreciate this." The conversation trailed off to family life and they said their goodbyes.

Amy's short period of consciousness was the only time she spoke during her stay in the hospital. She never woke again. Two days later, Amy's fight for life tragically ended when she succumbed to the trauma. A brain aneurism stopped the green monitor's white line from zigzagging. It lay flat. At the same time, the rhythmic beeping of the heart monitor changed to a constant high-pitched tone. Linda cried for help, for a nurse, for a doctor, for a miracle. They didn't make it in time.

After Amy's death, John was enraged and silently vowed, *My brother's not here to carry the banner of justice for Amy. But I am.*

***

Colter's Code

John believed open lines of communication solved conflicts by bringing people together to agree on common ground using give-and-take compromises. But he also recognized that throughout world history, there had existed evil people who chose to live by a different code, which was fueled by their consuming egos. They acted like kings who built their kingdoms of money and power on the pain and suffering of others. They wanted what other people possessed and took it by any means necessary, including stealing, beatings, torture, murder, and waging war. He knew evil people like Sal, who lived by that code, were only stopped by superior force and a violent end.

John also believed human behavior was produced by a complex combination of events and experiences. *Some are beyond our control, and others are controllable based on the choices each individual makes throughout their lives*, he thought. *You can't pick your parents, your siblings, or extended family. You can't control the country you were born in or the year, which dramatically influences your living conditions, culture, religion, and education. For example, what if you had been born into an African American family in Paris, Texas, in the 1920s or a Jewish family living in Poland in 1939?*

But we can control choices such as where we work, who our friends are, how hard we work, the level of education we achieve, our health through the food we eat and our level of exercise, the church we attend, and who we date and decide to marry.

John had made one of those life-changing choices in his first year of high school. He was eating lunch in the cafeteria with two classmates. The trio was constantly ridiculed and bullied for their obesity. Students called John names like Fatboy, Crusher, and Flubber Bucket. Flubber was a fictitious chemical compound with characteristics similar to a jellyfish created for a Disney movie. It was funny in a comedy movie but humiliating and degrading to John.

One day, he resolved to change his eating habits, and he began a rigorous exercise routine. Before long, he was healthier, leaner, and stronger, but the hurtful scars remained for the rest of his life. They were stored in a locked chamber in his memory only opened by painful reminders.

John's eighteenth birthday had been one of those uncontrollable life-changing events. The United States required men on their eighteenth birthday to register for the selective service military draft. It was held once a year, and each calendar day was assigned a lottery draft number. The lower the number assigned to a birthday, the higher the chance of selection. Conversely, the higher the number, the lower the chance. Men with calendar birthdates assigned a number below one hundred were guaranteed a trip to

Vietnam. If their numbers were above that, they were safe.

To set the stage, the uncensored independent news media brought the Vietnam War into the living rooms of every American family. Americans questioned why the war in Vietnam was necessary and when it would end. Those voices grew louder every night as the evening news broadcast listed the names of each young man killed, wounded, or missing during combat the previous day. Adding to the horror, the backdrop showed the images of dead bodies returning home in black boxes.

So, on that day, John was sitting on the dormitory lobby floor with his college friends anxiously watching the television screen. The announcer reached into a clear container filled with three hundred sixty-five floating lottery balls and plucked one randomly out of the air. He called out the number three for birthdate June 17. Panic overwhelmed John's friend Pat Turner. His birthdate was June 17. He enlisted in the navy the next day hoping to avoid Vietnam. John listened and waited until finally, the man announced his draft number. It was one hundred sixty-six.

Another life-changing event was influenced by random chance or fate. John's mother was mentally ill and unable to work. Child support and alimony from his deadbeat father were barely enough for food and shelter, and there was no extra money to pay for college. Jack joined the army with the hope of paying for college using the GI Bill. John found a job to earn his own money working after school as a busboy at a nearby Italian restaurant. He worked hard, and before long, he was promoted to a well-paying job as a waiter. Over the next two years, he saved enough money to enroll in an affordable college. *But where should I go?* he pondered.

Then, while researching colleges in the guidance office and at the recommendation of a friend, John reached for the Kansas State University's catalog. He soon realized he had grabbed the wrong book by mistake. He was reading about Kansas State College in Pittsburg, Kansas, an entirely different school. But he liked what he read, and two months later, he visited Pittsburg on a tour of midwestern colleges and decided to attend. There, he met Debbie, the love of his life.

Chapter 8
The Funeral

Linda's worst fear had come true, and hope turned to grief. The house in Maplewood became cold and dark. The warmth of Amy's smile that once brought sunshine to every room was extinguished forever. The contents of her bedroom soon would enter a new world stored away inside boxes, waiting for the white exterior cardboard to fade over the coming years to light brown.

John made the funeral arrangements at the Kingsley funeral home in Eltingville, on Staten Island. The Kingsleys were old family friends who had buried John's maternal grandparents at the Resthaven Cemetery in Great Kills. The Colter family owned a cemetery plot there for John's mother, Liv Larsen, next to her parents'. But her last will and testament requested to be cremated and then to have her ashes spread over the Hudson River Bay during a Staten Island Ferry crossing. She had worked as a model at the Bergdorf Goodman department store as a young girl and always cherished the ride to New York City. It was decided that Amy's grandmother's unused plot would be her final resting place.

The guests slowly arrived at the funeral home wearing their black attire and walked through the greeting area to share their condolences with Linda. They said things like, *We're so sorry for your loss.* Close acquaintances added words like, *Let us know how we can help* and *We'll miss her*. What else can someone say to a grieving mother whose daughter was murdered twelve days before her tenth birthday?

In the sanctuary, Amy Colter's body lay peacefully inside a small brown open casket with silver handles. Her mother had dressed her in a delicate white dress. Amy's arms held her favorite stuffed animal, Lammy. Each side of the casket was adorned with beautiful flower arrangements made of lilies, roses, orchids, carnations, and irises. A comforting fragrance filled the room.

Melancholy music softly filled the air as guests quietly sat in the pews.

John approached the casket and looked inside. His eyes watered as he bent over and gave Amy a soft kiss on the cheek. A teardrop fell from his face onto the white pillow that now held the little girl's delicate curls.

The image reminded John of when he held Amy's tiny hand at Jack's funeral. The confused little girl had looked up at him and asked why her daddy had left her and Mommy to live with the angels. John's mind jumped as he looked at Amy's placid face; he remembered a sunny spring day when he had pulled her in a red Radio Flyer wagon as their family strolled around Linda's neighborhood. A sad smile crossed his face when he reminisced about teaching her to ride a bicycle for the first time without training wheels. He had watched her zigzagging forward until confidently, the line straightened. She had been so happy.

He took a seat next to Linda and his family in the front row. He looked again at the casket. Then, his mind visualized Lady Justice, Justitia, immortalized in ancient Roman art, holding the scales of justice in her right hand while in her left hand holding the sword symbolizing punishment. He asked himself, *Will truth, justice, and fairness prevail to punish Amy's killers, or will the forces of evil win again?*

The somber gathering grew quiet as the funeral director began the service with words of welcome, comfort, and compassion.

A member of the Maplewood Presbyterian Church choir stood and sang the song "Borrowed Angels". It was a bittersweet reminder that Amy's life had ended too soon.

The church pastor rose from a seat behind the lectern to offer a message of God's hope and love while the listeners asked themselves, *Is there really a loving, caring God? If there is a God, how could God allow an innocent, beautiful, little girl to be killed so violently? How can the devil's minions triumph over good time and time again while God does nothing to stop it?*

John's attention came back to the scene in front of him, and he tuned into the end of the pastor's message.

"Amy's life ended before she could experience her first kiss and the fun of dancing at her senior prom. She won't cry tears of joy on her wedding day when her adoring, handsome husband lifts her white veil to kiss her. Nor will she cry in humility and awe when she holds her own baby after childbirth.

"No, my friends gathered here today for this solemn occasion. Amy won't experience a full life because it was callously cut short. You may ask God what good could come from this senseless act of violence. May I suggest this? Maybe death reminds us that every day God gives us is precious. As God tells us in Ecclesiastes 7:4, it is better to visit the house of mourning than of feasting. Let us live every day to the fullest."

Amy's cousin Ann Larsen stood and sang a somber song of hope. When she finished, John walked to the podium to give the eulogy. He looked across the overflowing room and said, "Thank you for coming today. I am Amy's Uncle John. I appreciate every one of you for taking time out of your lives to share today's memorial service for Amy.

"The joyful life of Amy started nine years ago at Women's Hospital in the Harlem neighborhood of New York City. It's the same hospital where her father Jack was born twenty-four years earlier. Jack is not with us physically today, but his spirit is. He is resting in the white stone gardens of Arlington National Cemetery.

"I remember when Amy was so excited on her third birthday because Daddy was home from Vietnam. They blew out the candles together and ate her favorite cake—white angel food with creamy chocolate frosting."

John gestured across the room. "When you entered the lobby today, you walked by a series of photographs depicting Amy's life. My favorite was taken by her mother Linda on a beach on Martha's Vineyard in Massachusetts. The image shows Jack holding Amy's hand as they walk along the beach at sunset while a shiny blue wave licks the gray sand. Their backs are toward the camera, creating a silhouette against the orange skyline dotted with oblong gray clouds, suspended across the light-blue horizon.

"Amy's teachers told Linda at a parent-teacher conference that Amy's smile lit up the classroom. She was always kind and helping other students." His voice broke at the memory, and John choked back tears.

"I asked her friends what they liked best about Amy. They said she made them laugh.

"My wife, Debbie, shared the story of a girls' slumber party when Amy visited our home in Pittsburg. She said Amy and my daughter were laughing so hard, at whatever little girls laugh at, they were crying and yelling, 'Stop. Stop! I can't breathe.' Doesn't that sound like fun? She was such a joyful child.

"Our time with Amy was filled with so many memorable moments that it is hard to share only a special few. One night while our family was camping at Lake George, we were sitting around the campfire and decided to make some s'mores. Shortly thereafter, all eyes turned toward Amy as we watched her first attempt at cooking a marshmallow. The spongy white confection overheated, started melting, and caught fire. She frowned in frustration as it fell into the flaming logs, and I asked, 'Amy, can I help you?'

"Then she gave me her determined look. The one she'd learned from her mother. I helped her skewer a fresh marshmallow onto the small, sharpened stick. Minutes later, Amy sat in triumph on a wooden log eating the tasty graham cracker filled with Hershey's chocolate and the toasted marshmallow. S'mores were now her favorite dessert. We were mesmerized by her excitement as the intermittent light from the flames danced across her face.

"She said, 'Thank you, Uncle John,' and she joyfully jumped up to give me a big hug and soft kiss on the cheek. I melted like one of those marshmallows.

"The next night, we were tucked away in our cozy sleeping bags and the sound of the tent zipper opening

Colter's Code

interrupted the quiet. Moments later, Amy's voice shouted in the darkness: 'Give me that.'

"Linda pointed a flashlight toward Amy's voice and to everyone's surprise, there was Amy gripping the end of a loaf of bread. A raccoon was pulling the opposite end. The tug-of-war ended when Linda grabbed a sneaker and hurled it at the brazen intruder. Amy victoriously held the bread in her hands. We watched in amazement as the raccoon darted out the unzipped doorway. We followed to catch the culprit, but the forest wouldn't reveal its hiding place. Then Linda had an idea that solved the mystery. Linda searched the trees above the campsite with her flashlight. There he was, but he was not alone. The raccoon and its nursery of cute companions were laughing at us from the tree limbs above.

"The sound of Amy's laughter will never bring us joy again. Her smile won't light up the room. Her hugs and kisses are not here to bring tears to my eyes. But I will tell you this: I will always cherish the memories of my niece Amy. On the coldest and darkest days, the thought of her gentle spirit will always warm my heart.

"Linda drew a line on the kitchen wall each year on Amy's birthday to record her growing taller. Maybe some of you draw the same line by the refrigerator at your house and record the joy of your children growing into adulthood. The top line for Jack was six feet, three inches. The last line for Amy was four feet, eight inches. Her line will never move any higher.

"In closing, let me say this to each of you. Remember fondly those you loved who no longer share our journey. Let their memories inspire you to live a more fulfilling life. Each of us celebrates our birthdays, and we should, but also ask yourself this: How many more birthdays do I have remaining before I join Amy? What choices will I make today to enjoy the day, and what can I do to help my family and friends live a better life?"

John returned to join his family while Ann sang the final song, "Somewhere Over the Rainbow," Amy's favorite from *The Wizard of Oz*.

The funeral procession of vehicles was outlined by New York City police motorcycles driving from the funeral home to the cemetery for the final service. The hearse quietly rolled to a stop beside the black tent that covered the gravesite. Pastel-gray storm clouds rolled against the blue sky. Umbrellas snapped into their protective positions, sending the pitter-patter sound of raindrops bouncing off their half-moon shields. Beside the grave, the large crowd of men and women wearing their black suits and dark dresses surrounded the family who were sitting on folding chairs in front of the casket. The funeral director shared comforting words, and then each family member and guest placed one white rose on the semicircular black top of the casket. The service ended with the pallbearers lowering Amy's casket into the ground beside her great-grandfather and great-grandmother, those two courageous Norwegians who, many years earlier, had sailed into New York Harbor past the Statue of Liberty to build a new life in America.

Chapter 9
The Arrest

The public outcry for justice was ignited by the news media who published sensational stories about the tragic killing of a nine-year-old little girl while she was playing in her bedroom. To add fuel to the fire, they printed a picture of her faithful dog, Max, who was found dead by her side. They had been innocent victims caught in the crossfire of two mobsters firing high-powered shotguns at an empty van parked in the street. Its owner had been out of town on a fishing trip.

Behind the scenes, the FBI's Organized Crime Division applied pressure on the Essex County District Attorney to arrest and convict Sal and Joey for the murder. The government needed a win against the Mafia after suffering too many defeats. But the strongest pressure was applied by Superior Court Judge John Marshall. His granddaughter, Ruth, had been best friends with Amy, and she had asked her grandpa one day, "Will the bad men who hurt Amy be punished?" Judge Marshall was enraged and within an hour was on the phone demanding the perpetrators be brought to justice.

The criminal investigation gained momentum as the detectives gathered evidence to build their case. In the process, Henry Carlson signed his witness statement at the Maplewood Police Station. And after the meeting, Detective O'Keefe asked Carlson, "Do you have any concerns or fears that the Mafia may intimidate you or kill you to prevent your testimony?"

Carlson laughed and said, "Hell no. After killing Japanese in the jungles during World War II, I'm not afraid of anybody! You learned to kill without remorse to survive. Let me ask you something, detective. Have you ever seen what a Colt .45 pistol does to a man's head at point-blank range?

"I'd kill any one of those Mafia scum for Amy without hesitation. I can do it from a distance with a rifle, or up close and personal with a pistol. Hell, if I wanted to, I could do it silently using a knife or with my bare hands."

Eventually, the time came when Essex County District Attorney David Fox decided he had collected sufficient evidence to prove the shooting was premeditated and that second-degree manslaughter was a provable charge. Sal and Joey had acted recklessly and were fully aware of the outcome of their actions.

Fox issued arrest warrants and called defense lawyer Lautenberg as a courtesy to request that he bring his clients to the Maplewood Police Station for processing. When they arrived, the accused were fingerprinted, photographed, and moved to a holding cell to wait for the arraignment.

Before long, Sal and Joey were escorted into the courtroom to the defense table to sit with their lawyers, Lautenberg and his assistant Roger Bailey.

Municipal Court Judge Longstreet looked up and announced, "Salvatore Provenzano, you are accused of second-degree manslaughter in the death of Amy Colter. What is your plea?"

Standing, Sal answered, "Not guilty, Your Honor."

The judge turned to Joey and said, "Joseph Provenzano, you are accused of second-degree manslaughter in the death of Amy Colter. What is your plea?"

Joey said, "Not guilty, Your Honor."

Judge Longstreet asked, "Mr. Fox, what is the State's recommendation for bail in this case?"

Fox responded, "Your Honor, the people of the State of New Jersey ask that bail be set at $250,000 for Salvatore Provenzano and $250,000 for Joseph Provenzano."

Mr. Lautenberg responded, "Your Honor, my clients do not have criminal records and are not flight risks. They were born in New York City and have lived in the metropolitan area of New York City their whole lives. Salvatore is gainfully employed as a vice president of the local Teamsters Union. Joseph is gainfully employed as a project foreman by the Summit Concrete Company. Their families live here, and they are prominent members of the local community. Therefore, my clients respectfully request bail at a reduced amount."

Judge Longstreet ordered, "Bail is set at $100,000 for each of the defendants. You're dismissed. Next case."

The wheels of the justice system moved quickly, and the preliminary hearing was held the following week at Lautenberg's request. The official record of those in attendance included the judge, District Attorney Fox, Assistant District Attorney Condon, Defense Lawyer Lautenberg, Bailey, the county clerk, the court reporter, Sal, and Joey.

The prosecution presented forensic evidence and testimony from two witnesses to establish probable cause. The evidence demonstrated the commission of a crime took place when the defendants fired shotguns into the parked van and the Colters' house across the street resulting in the subsequent death of Amy Colter.

The judge ruled that the evidence met the standard of a *prima facie* case for the State of New Jersey. Then, he announced that the trial would be held in Judge Newell's court on a date scheduled by that court. His final order released the defendants pursuant to their bail agreements.

The day of the trial arrived. Presiding Judge David Newell welcomed the prospective jurors chosen from the Essex County, New Jersey, registered voter records, and then gave instructions about the process for jury selection in a criminal trial.

He began by saying, "Today, you will be asked questions by the lawyers for the prosecution and defense. Please answer their questions truthfully. Our goal is to select twelve final jurors and two alternates to conduct a fair and impartial trial as established by the Sixth Amendment to the Constitution of the United States. If you are selected, you have the honor and privilege of serving your community. The trial may last several weeks, during which time you may be sequestered in a hotel room. If for any reason you cannot serve for an extended length of time, please tell me now.

"The lawyers may not select you to participate in this trial. Lawyers have what are called challenges, which means they can ask me to excuse you from serving. Please do not take it personally. Hundreds of potential jurors just like you are excused in my court every year.

"As a prospective juror, you were required to complete the juror qualifications questionnaire. The court sent copies to District Attorney Fox and Defense Lawyer Lautenberg. They're indexed in those black binders you see sitting on their tables. In addition to those questionnaires, it's common for both the district attorney's staff and the defense staff to research additional background information on each of you."

After the judge's instructions, the lawyers started questioning the prospective jurors based on a detailed personality analysis prepared for each individual. As part of that process, Fox and Lautenberg had hired separate consulting firms with expertise in designing questions using the Myers-Briggs psychological study to ferret out jurors favorable to their point of view.

Two days later, the prosecution and defense notified the judge they were satisfied with the jury. Fox called John to inform him that the trial was going to begin the following Monday.

With the trial date set, John and Debbie booked a flight from Kansas City to Newark Airport. As their Boeing 727 approached Newark Airport, John looked out the window at the Meadowlands and noticed the new Giants football stadium below. It reminded John of the day his father had brought Jack and him to Yankee Stadium to watch a live Giants football game for the first time.

His dad had purchased the tickets to the Sunday afternoon game against the Philadelphia Eagles though work connections at the Radio Corporation of America, RCA. The tickets included lunch at the exclusive Yankee Stadium club restaurant, which was a special treat for two young, impressionable boys like Jack and John. Adding to the excitement, Joe Namath, the superstar playboy quarterback of the New York

Jets, sat down at the table next to the boys. Of course, he was accompanied by two beautiful blondes.

John had two idols growing up. One was Mickey Mantle, the all-star outfielder for the New York Yankees who had replaced Joe DiMaggio in center field. The other was Joe Willie Namath. John was in football heaven.

Jack knew John idolized Broadway Joe, but his little brother was too scared to get up and meet the legend. So, Jack grabbed John by the arm and pushed him toward Joe's table.

Then he said, "Mr. Namath. Can we have your autograph?"

"Absolutely, young man. Who should I address it too?" Namath asked.

"It for my little brother, John. You're his idol."

Joe signed John's brown football-shaped children's menu.

Jack thanked Mr. Namath for the autograph and shook his hand.

John stood speechless, but managed a soft, "Thank you Mr. Namath," and smiled as big as a sickle moon.

One of the striking blondes kissed John on the cheek and said, "What a little darling."

John turned as bright red as her luscious lipstick as every adult male in the room watched with envy. He didn't wash the kiss imprint off his cheek for days.

John fondly remembered Jack's love and kindness. His heart missed his big brother.

The trial started Monday as scheduled, on the second floor of the Superior Court of New Jersey, Law Division Essex County, located on Martin Luther King Jr. Boulevard in Newark, New Jersey.

Linda sat behind the prosecution table in a black dress. Her outfit was a symbol to the jury of her grief and loss. John and Debbie sat beside her, accompanied by Marine Colonel Andy Hackworth, Jack's commanding officer in Vietnam. John had asked the colonel to attend the trial to honor his fallen friend. The colonel's chest, decorated with military bars and medals, sent a powerful message to the jury of the sacrifice the victim's father had made defending his country.

Soft whispers rose to incessant chatter as reporters, family, friends, Genovese crime family members, and interested spectators filled the gallery.

After the ceremonial "Please rise" and announcements by the court clerk, Judge Newell swore in the standing jurors, saying, "Please raise your right hand. Do you, the jury, solemnly swear or affirm you will objectively listen to the evidence presented in this case, render a just verdict in accordance with the laws of the State of New Jersey, and recommend a fair sentence as to the defendants, so help you God?"

Each juror answered, "I do."

Newell responded to the group, "Please be seated."

He turned to Fox and asked, "Is the prosecution ready?"

Fox answered, "The State is ready, Your Honor."

Next, Newell asked Lautenberg, "Is the defense ready?" After his affirmation, the judge instructed the prosecution to present its opening statement.

Chapter 10
The Trial

District Attorney Fox stood in front of the jury box to deliver his opening remarks and said, "Good morning, ladies and gentlemen of the jury. You are here today to represent a little girl named Amy Colter. Nine-year-old Amy is not present today because she is buried next to her great-grandma and great-grandpa Larsen over on Staten Island. Amy's young life ended with a senseless act of violence by the two men you see sitting right there." He pointed. "Their names are Salvatore Provenzano and Joseph Provenzano. During this trial, the State will present a preponderance of clear and convincing evidence that proves beyond a reasonable doubt that Salvatore and Joseph committed second-degree manslaughter when their actions caused Amy's death. Did this little girl provoke or threaten these men? No, my friends. She was innocently playing in her bedroom. The police also found her dog, Max. His bullet-riddled body lay faithfully beside her.

"You may ask yourself why these two men aren't charged with first-degree murder? Well, under the law, they did not plan to kill Amy, so it was not premeditated. But the State will prove based on the evidence presented Sal and Joey's reckless actions killed Amy. That is second-degree manslaughter. The defense will claim it was an accident that occurred while Sal and Joey were defending themselves from an assassin. The problem with that defense is they knowingly and willfully fired high-powered shotguns and destroyed the van parked outside their house. Then, they reloaded and fired again and again. Why?

"They watched the van for hours that day, and no one threatened them. If they suspected they were in danger and believed they would be attacked, why didn't they call the police? I'll tell you why. They decided to take the law into their own hands. Their clear intention was to murder the occupants of the van. The law and civilized societies do not allow citizens to shoot and kill other people or destroy property based on the assumption that their lives are threatened by an imaginary assassin hiding in a van parked in the street. The fact is the van was empty. There was no threat, and there was no reason to destroy the empty van. The shotgun shells they used were so powerful, the pellets penetrated the walls of the Colters' house across the street and killed Amy."

When Fox was finished, Lautenberg stood and confidently walked to the jury box to present the opening statement in defense of Sal and Joey. He was wearing a meticulously tailored black suit with a blue tie. The shine of his black shoes sparkled. He looked very distinguished, like Gregory Peck in the movie *To Kill a Mockingbird*.

Then he began by saying in a soothing voice, "Good morning, ladies and gentlemen of the jury." He

Colter's Code

looked each one of them in the eyes as he spoke, walking purposely in front of the jury box. "Thank you for serving on the jury. Trials are based on the facts presented as real evidence, not circumstantial evidence based on speculation. If the prosecution fails to present a fact in this trial, then in the eyes of the law, the fact does not exist. Compounding the problem is that humans, during times of great stress, do not always remember what they actually saw or heard. During this trial, you will see and hear very disturbing, even shocking, evidence. That's why I'm asking you to carefully listen to the testimony and presentation of the facts and ask yourself, 'Is there corroborating testimony and facts?' For example, only one State witness will testify that he thought he recognized Sal and Joey shooting shotguns from their living room window.

"I am sure the witness is a good man trying to do his best to remember what he saw. But the problem is, the State doesn't have another witness to confirm those alleged facts. Is it possible this neighbor did not see Sal or Joey, but actually witnessed two similar-looking men in the living room window? Is it possible the man's memory distorted the truth? Ask yourself, did the elderly witness have an early form of dementia? Was his eyesight failing with age? Was he frightened by exploding gunshots and get confused? Is it possible that because Sal lives in that house, this witness expected to see Sal in the window, so his mind only *thinks* he saw Sal?

"Another problem for the prosecution is they don't have the shotguns used to commit the crime. The police searched inside the Provenzano house and found no physical evidence linking the weapons used in this crime to the Provenzanos."

After Lautenberg was satisfied that he had planted sufficient seeds of doubt, he concluded his opening statement.

Judge Newell ordered a fifteen-minute recess and when the court was back in session, he asked Prosecutor Fox to call his first witness.

Fox announced, "The State calls Maplewood Patrolman William Wagner as its first witness, Your Honor."

The judge said to Patrolman Wagner, "Please raise your right hand, and place your left hand on this bible. Do you swear to tell the truth, the whole truth, and nothing but the truth, so help you God?"

Wagner responded, "I do."

Attorney Fox began his questions to establish for the record the credibility of the witness. He asked, "Mr. Wagner, would you please state your full name and occupation, then describe your training and experience."

Wagner answered, "My name is William Edward Wagner. I attended the Essex County Police Academy.

After graduation, I worked for two years as a patrolman for the Newark, New Jersey, Police Department. The last four years, I've worked as a patrolman in Maplewood."

"Thank you, Detective Wagner. Were you one of the two patrolmen who first arrived at the crime scene the day of the shooting?" Fox said.

Patrolman Wagner answered, "Yes, I was."

Fox asked, "Can you describe for the jury what you observed when you arrived that day?"

Wagner answered, "My partner, Patrick Connolly, and I responded to a radio call to investigate gunshots fired at 181 Norfolk Street in Maplewood. When we drove to that address, we noticed a van parked in the street all shot to pieces, so we exited our vehicle to investigate. First, we looked up and down the street but didn't see anybody."

"What happened next?" Fox said.

Wagner replied, "We searched the van and thankfully, nobody was inside. There were bullet holes everywhere. Then, we noticed some smoke lingering in front of the house at 181. There wasn't any wind that day, so it was just hanging there in the air."

Fox asked, "What did the smoke smell like?"

Wagner said, "It smelled like gunpowder."

Fox asked, "Did you walk over to the house to investigate?"

Wagner answered, "Well. We were going to, but we noticed a broken window at the Colters' and went to check it out. As we got closer, we saw some bullet holes in the front of the house and then heard the faint sound of crying through a downstairs window.

"We proceeded to the front door, where I knocked and announced who I was, then I shouted, 'Is anyone home?' An older man answered and introduced himself as Henry Carlson. He was the next-door neighbor. Mr. Carlson escorted us downstairs to Amy Colter's room, where we found Mrs. Colter, Amy, and their dog."

Fox replied, "That must have been an awful sight." He paused to give the jury time to visualize the room. "Please describe for the jury what you witnessed inside Amy's bedroom."

Wagner turned toward the jury and summarized the gruesome scene.

Fox concluded his questions for Patrolman Wagner by saying, "Thank you, officer." Turning to the judge, he said, "Your Honor, I have no more questions."

Lautenberg stood to cross-examine and said, "Your Honor, I have a few questions for Patrolman Wagner. Patrolman Wagner, you said you observed smoke in the air in front of the Provenzanos' house. Did the smoke obstruct your view of the front living room window of the house at 181 Norfolk Street?"

Patrolman Wagner paused to think, then replied, "Yes, a little."

Lautenberg asked, "Did you see anyone in the window?"

Wagner replied, "No, sir. I did not."

"No further questions at this time, Your Honor." Lautenberg said.

Judge Newell announced, "Mr. Fox, you may call your next witness."

"Your Honor, the State calls Officer Patrick Connolly to the witness stand," Fox said.

The judge concluded the swearing in of the witness, and Fox asked the standard questions about his credentials and employment to establish him as a credible witness. Then asked, "Officer Connolly, were you one of the two police officers who arrived first on the scene at the Colters' house?"

Connolly replied, "Yes. I was."

Fox said, "Officer Connolly. Is it true the sight of Amy's Colter's bullet-ravaged body was so revolting that you immediately had to exit the house to throw up outside in the grass?"

Connolly answered, "Yes, sir. That is true."

"And why was it so upsetting?" Fox asked.

"I have two young daughters about Amy's age, and when I saw her body lying on the floor like that, I got so nauseated, I just had to get some fresh air and calm down."

Mark E. Uhler

Fox concluded his questions, and the witness was excused. Then he went to the prosecution's table, reviewed his yellow notepad, and said, "Your Honor, the State calls Kent Lancaster to the stand."

After Lancaster was sworn in by Judge Newell, Fox said, "Mr. Lancaster, please state your name and occupation."

Lancaster answered, "My name is Kent Lancaster. I am the lead forensic scientist employed by the State of New Jersey at the criminal investigation laboratory located in Trenton, New Jersey."

Fox said, "Mr. Lancaster, what is your educational background and how long have you worked in the state police crime lab?"

Lancaster replied, "I graduated from Hofstra University in Hempstead, New York, on Long Island with a bachelor's degree and master's degree in forensic sciences and pathology. After graduation, I was hired by the crime laboratory for the State of New York. I worked there six years and then was hired by the crime laboratory in Trenton. I've worked there for the last sixteen years."

Fox asked, "Mr. Lancaster, have you published any articles as an expert in forensic science?"

Lancaster answered, "Yes. Six of my papers were accepted for publication in the *Journal of Forensic Sciences*."

Fox said, "That's very impressive, Mr. Lancaster. Did you examine the evidence from the crime scene?"

He responded, "Yes, I did."

Fox proceeded to submit exhibits into evidence and asked Lancaster to describe what they were and how they were related to the case. Then, he paused his questions to retrieve a critical bag of evidence from his table, turned to the judge, and said, "Your Honor, the State enters the following exhibit from Amy Colter's bedroom into evidence."

Next, Fox asked Mr. Lancaster, "What are these white-and-pink pieces of material retrieved from Amy Colter's room?"

Lancaster answered, "These particles are pieces of Amy's flesh, bone, and brain matter."

Fox said, "Thank you, Mr. Lancaster. Please tell the jury what violent act caused her body to be torn apart like that."

Lancaster replied, "We retrieved thirteen double-aught lead pellets from her bedroom. Four of those penetrated her body with such force that they traveled through her flesh and bone and exited the other side."

Fox asked, "Were these pellets from what is referred to as a 'tactical round,' and if so, what are they used for?"

Lancaster testified, "Yes, the pellets originated from high-powered tactical shotgun shells. The shells are designed to create maximum damage to the target.

Double-aught pellets are the largest pellets manufactured for shotgun shells. Law enforcement personnel and Special Forces in the military use the rounds to neutralize people who are threats—in effect, to kill them quickly."

Fox changed his line of questioning and asked, "Moving on to the outside of the house, what were your conclusions from your examination of the van?"

Lancaster answered, "The force of the lead pellets was so powerful, the metal walls were shredded and the glass windows shattered."

Fox concluded by saying, "Your Honor, I have no more questions for the State's expert witness."

Lautenberg rose and said, "Your Honor. The defense has no questions for the witness at this time but reserves the right to cross-examine Mr. Lancaster at a future date."

The judge looked at the weary jury. Their body language projected the message that they were unable to digest more evidence. He ordered a two-hour recess for lunch to allow them time to clear their minds.

John approached Attorney Fox at the Courtroom Café across the street and asked, "Why do Sal and Joey appear so confident? They look like they don't have a care in the world. They certainly don't act worried like two men on trial for manslaughter."

Fox admitted, "They do look very confident. It's like they know the jury's verdict, even before the jury hears all the evidence and renders a decision."

Following the lunch break, Fox called the next witness. "The State calls Henry Carlson to the stand. Mr. Carlson, thank you for coming today. Would you please state your name for the record, discuss your background, and describe what you witnessed the day of Amy Colter's murder?"

Carlson coughed twice, cleared his throat, and began. "My name is Henry Carlson, and I live next door to the Colters' house. I recently retired from the Prudential Insurance Company in Newark, where I worked as an actuary for twenty-six years. I was home watching an afternoon Yankees game on WPIX when I heard the sound of gunshots. I jumped up to look outside to find out what the hell was going on out there. When I looked out the living room window, I saw two men across the street firing shotguns at the van parked in the street."

Fox asked, "How did you know the two men were firing shotguns?"

Carlson answered, "I know what a shotgun looks like and sounds like. The Marine Corps gave us extensive training on how to identify different weapons from their sight and sound before we shipped out to the Pacific in World War II. There, you get your PhD in lethal weapons in the heat of battle, surrounded in the jungle by the Japanese who are trying to kill you."

Fox responded, "Mr. Carlson, can you positively identify the two men firing the shotguns from the window across the street at the Provenzano house?"

Carlson replied, "Yes, I can. They are sitting right there." Pointing, he added, "That's my neighbor Sal Provenzano and his son Joey."

Attorney Lautenberg had explained to Sal before the trial that Mr. Carlson was a decorated war hero, and he would be a credible witness. Sal had contemplated preventing Carlson's testimony through the usual methods of bribery or intimidation. He had even considered sending him on a permanent vacation wearing cement shoes but decided it would bring too much scrutiny. In the end, Sal trusted Lautenberg's strategy to mitigate his testimony by discrediting the witness. If that didn't work? Well, they had other ways of winning a not-guilty verdict.

Fox then asked, "What did you do next?"

Carlson replied, "I went out the front door to check out the van. When I did, I noticed a broken downstairs window at the Colters'. As I got closer, I heard the faint sound of crying coming out of it, so I hurried over to the front door. I knocked feverishly, but no one answered. Then, I yelled, 'Linda, is everyone OK in there?' I didn't hear an answer, so I went inside. That's when I found Mrs. Colter downstairs, holding Amy in her arms, rocking her back and forth sobbing. It was a terrible sight."

At the conclusion of Fox's questioning, Judge Newell asked, "Mr. Lautenberg, would you like to cross-examine the witness?"

Lautenberg stood up and said, "Yes, Your Honor."

He approached the witness stand and said, "Mr. Carlson. Thank you for your service in the Marines; you're an American hero. May I ask how old you are?"

Carlson answered, "I'm sixty-eight years old."

Lautenberg placed a finger on his lips, paused, and replied, "I am going to ask you a few more questions to help the jury understand what you saw that day. Were you nervous or afraid?"

Carlson said, "No, sir. As I said before to Mr. Fox, I fought in the jungles of Guadalcanal; I am not afraid of gunshots. You learned to control your fear or you died."

Lautenberg continued, "Mr. Carlson, the Department of Motor Vehicles records indicate your driver's license requires you to wear glasses when you drive. Can you see objects far away without your glasses?"

Carlson replied, "Yes, but they're a little blurry."

Lautenberg inquisitively said, "So, if you saw a person, let's say, visiting Mrs. Walker's house across the street from yours, and you were not wearing your prescription glasses, would you recognize the details of their face?"

Carlson answered, "No, sir."

Lautenberg asked, "Were you wearing your glasses the day you were watching the Yankees game?"

Carlson responded, "Yes, sir. The television channels are a little blurry without them, so I put them on to watch the game. You can ask one of those policemen. They saw me wearing my glasses."

Now that Lautenberg had set up his strategy, he said, "That won't be necessary, Mr. Carlson. Let me ask you this. When was the last time you visited the eye doctor to have your vision examined?"

Curtly, Carlson answered, "I can see just fine with my glasses. I don't need to go to any eye doctor. You can get one of those eyecharts, if you want, and put it against that wall, and I'll prove I see good enough with them on."

Lautenberg asked his next question. "Mr. Carlson, the official records from your eye doctor's office showed your last visit was three years ago. Is that correct?"

He responded, "I guess so. If that's what it says."

Lautenberg quickly asked, "Have you visited any other eye doctor since that visit?"

Carlson replied, "No. I haven't."

"So, you admit that you do not have a current prescription and that you have difficulty seeing details without your corrective lenses." Lautenberg abruptly said before Carlson could answer, "Thank you, Mr. Carlson. Judge, I have no further questions for the witness at this time."

Judge Newell turned to the witness stand and said, "You're excused, Mr. Carlson. Thank you for your testimony. Mr. Fox, please call your next witness."

"Your Honor, the prosecution calls Detective Robert O'Keefe to the stand."

After Fox asked Detective O'Keefe to state his name, occupation, and experience for the record, he asked, "Mr. O'Keefe, were you the lead detective called to the scene of the Amy Colter murder?"

He answered, "Yes. I was."

Fox said, "Please describe for the jury the events that took place after you arrived."

O'Keefe replied, "My partner, Shaun Murphy, and I walked over to Officers Wagner and Connolly to ask for a summary of what happened. After they discussed what they found, Murphy and I inspected the van."

Fox asked, "Did you find any blood, clothing, weapons, ammunition, or any other evidence indicating there had been assassins hiding in the van?"

O'Keefe answered, "No, sir, we did not."

Fox said in a bold tone, "Did you find anything threatening in the van that would have created enough fear in a reasonable person to lead them to believe they were in imminent danger of being attacked or killed?"

O'Keefe firmly said, "No, sir. We did not."

Fox said, "Thank you. Please continue. What did you do after you inspected the empty van?"

O'Keefe replied, "After we completed our examination of the van, we went to investigate what had happened at the Colter house. Inside Amy's bedroom we found the paramedics performing first aid on her as a result of multiple gunshot wounds. Her mother, Linda, was beside her, watching the paramedics. Their dog Max was lying on the floor next to Amy. He was deceased as the result of gunshot wounds. When the police photographer arrived, we coordinated the gathering and bagging of evidence while he took pictures."

Fox ended his questioning of O'Keefe, and Lautenberg stood to cross-examine. He paced the room with his hands behind his back and said, "Detective O'Keefe, were you part of the team that searched the Provenzano residence?"

O'Keefe answered, "Yes, I was."

Lautenberg asked, "Did you find any weapons at the house?"

O'Keefe, replied, "Yes. In the basement, we found two Smith & Wesson revolvers, a Remington 30-06 rifle, and a BAR—that's Browning Automatic Rifle."

Lautenberg asked, "Did you find any shotguns?"

O'Keefe said, "No, sir. We did not."

Without a pause, Lautenberg asked, "Did you find any shotguns shells—more specifically, any shotgun shells loaded with double-aught buckshot pellets?"

O'Keefe leaned forward in the witness chair and responded, "No, sir. We did not."

"Thank you. That concludes my questions for Detective O'Keefe, Your Honor," Lautenberg said.

Fox leaped from the prosecutor's table with purpose. "Redirect, Your Honor?"

Judge Newell said, "Go ahead."

Fox asked, "Detective O'Keefe, did you search the Provenzanos' house the day Amy Colter was shot?"

O'Keefe answered, "No, sir. We did not."

Fox asked inquisitively, "Why not?"

O'Keefe replied, "Mr. Provenzano's lawyer, Mr. Lautenberg, was present. He informed us Mr. Provenzano was very upset by the shooting and had drunk some Scotch whisky to calm his nerves. Mr. Lautenberg asked us to conduct the interview later."

Fox intensified his tone. "That doesn't answer the question. Why didn't you search the house that day?"

O'Keefe answered, "We asked for permission to enter the residence, but Mr. Lautenberg declined on behalf of his client. Then he asked if we had a search warrant. We did not, and we left to obtain one from a judge."

Fox was frustrated that the detectives had not searched the house the day of the shooting to find critical evidence such as the shotguns and ammunition. What Fox didn't know was Sal had ordered Bruno to dispose of the shotguns before the detectives arrived at the door. Exasperated, Fox said, "You're an experienced detective. Irrespective of permission, didn't you know you already had sufficient probable cause to search the house?"

O'Keefe defended his actions by saying, "No, sir. When Attorney Lautenberg denied entry, I didn't think it would be legal without a search warrant signed by a judge."

Fox asked, "When did you finally search the Provenzanos' house?"

O'Keefe answered, "The following day, we—"

Fox interrupted and said, "Did Sal Provenzano have enough time to dispose of two shotguns and the ammunition at any time between when you left his house the day of the murder and when you returned the next day?"

Lautenberg stood and said, "Objection, Your Honor: the question calls for speculation."

Judge Newell said, "Sustained. Detective O'Keefe, do not answer that question."

But it was too late for the defense. Fox had planted the question he wanted the jury to hear. "No more questions, Your Honor," he said.

Chapter 11
The Star Witness

Judge Newell entered the packed courtroom from his private chambers at nine in the morning the next day. The court clerk announced, "All rise. The court of the Honorable Judge David Newell is now in session."

Judge Newell sat at his bench and asked Prosecutor Fox to call his first witness of the day.

Fox began by stating, "Your Honor, the State calls Dr. William Brewer to the witness stand."

The judge proceeded to swear in the witness.

Fox then said, "Dr. Brewer, please state your name and occupation for the jury."

"My name is William Brewer. I am a professor at Pennsylvania State University, where I teach various forensic science courses designed to educate students on how to apply scientific principles and methods to assist criminal investigations. Pertinent to my testimony today, in my physics class, I teach the effects of ballistics on physical objects. In my chemistry class, I teach the analysis of gunshot residue."

Fox asked additional questions to establish Dr. Brewer as the leading ballistics scientist in the United States. When Fox was satisfied with the answers, he said, "Dr. Brewer, please describe for the jury the physical damage double-aught buckshot pellets do to metal when fired from a shotgun. Specifically in this case, the damage to the parked van."

Dr. Brewer began a detailed response: "The shotgun is the ultimate weapon for personal or home defense. The firing chamber launches a group of lead balls called shot down the barrel. After the shot—in this case, the double-aught pellets—exit the barrel, they start out in a close pattern, a line if you will. The farther they travel, the more they expand into a wider group or pattern. As you can see from the pictures of the van, the powerful force of the pellets caused them to perforate the metal walls and shatter the windows. Inside the van, the pellets ripped apart the dashboard and shredded the seats along with the other contents. Everything was destroyed.

"The tactical load double-aught buckshot pellets measure point, thirty-three calibers. A standard shell is two point seven-five inches long and contains nine pellets. These shells are designed for gunfights because of their devastating power through pellet size, spread pattern, and penetration. For example, the size and force of shells containing buckshot number-four pellets, which measure point twenty-four calibers and contain twenty-seven pellets per shell, will kill a German shepherd dog weighing sixty-five pounds at a distance of fifty yards."

Brewer paused to read the jury's faces to see if they were following. Most were nodding their heads, a clear sign they understood. Then he added, "In the laboratory at Pennsylvania State University, for this trial my team of scientists constructed a replica of the exterior wall of the Colter house using the exact same building materials. On the inside, the team built a replica of Amy's bedroom. Then, they placed a mannequin made of ballistic gelatin into the room that was the exact size and weight of Amy.

"The next step was to reenact the gunshots, so they fired shotgun shells loaded with double-aught buckshot from a twelve-gauge shotgun at a distance of thirty-two yards. That was the exact distance from the Provenzanos' living room window. Six of the nine pellets loaded in the shell casing penetrated the outside walls of the house and traveled through the gelatin."

Fox said, "Thank you, Dr. Brewer. Who uses tactical double-aught buckshot shells and why do they use them?"

Dr. Brewer answered, "Law enforcement officials use double-aught buckshot shells to neutralize violent criminals posing a serious threat."

Fox asked, "Would you use shells containing double-aught pellets for killing, let us say, a goose while hunting?" He picked up a large live goose as a visual aid. On cue like in a comedy movie, the frightened goose crapped all over the courtroom floor. The crowded room erupted in laughter. Fortunately, the stream shooting out of the goose's back end missed Fox's well-pressed business suit.

The judge ordered a recess to clean up the mess and allow the bedlam to subside.

When the trial continued, Dr. Brewer answered, "No, the power and size of double-aught pellets would tear apart the bird. There's a tradeoff. Smaller pellets have less killing force, but there are more pellets to do the job. The larger the pellet size, the fewer the number of pellets but the greater the killing power."

Fox looked at his list of questions and said, "Can we conclude that double-aught–sized pellets fired from a shotgun at a distance of thirty-two yards would kill a little girl the size of Amy?"

Lautenberg stood, "Objection, Your Honor. Speculation on the part of the witness."

Judge Newell, "I'll allow the question. Dr. Brewer is the leading expert in the United States. Dr. Brewer, please answer Mr. Fox's question."

Fox repeated the question. "Dr. Brewer, as a ballistics expert specializing in the damage to the human body from gunshots wounds, in your opinion, would double-aught pellets fired from a shotgun at thirty-two yards have enough force to travel through the wall of the Colter house and kill Amy Colter?"

Dr. Brewer answered emphatically, "Yes. The pellets would contain sufficient force to penetrate the walls of the Colter house and travel though Amy's body."

Fox ended by saying, "No further questions for the witness, Your Honor."

Judge Newell said, "Court is in recess for a one-hour lunch break."

After the break, Fox announced, "Your Honor, the prosecution calls Dr. David Schaeffer to the stand."

After the doctor was sworn in, Fox said, "Please state your name and credentials for the record."

The doctor answered, "My name is Dr. David Schaeffer; I am a surgeon with credentials at College Hospital in Newark, New Jersey. I graduated from the Harvard University School of Biology and Harvard Medical School in Cambridge, Massachusetts. I completed my residency requirements at Massachusetts General Hospital in Boston and then worked at Mass General as an emergency room trauma surgeon. After two years, I decided to serve our country by helping the noble wounded warriors in Vietnam, and I resigned my position to enlist in the United States Army. There, I was a surgeon in a mobile army surgical hospital, a MASH unit. After my honorable discharge from the army, I accepted a surgical position at College Hospital in Newark."

Fox asked Dr. Schaeffer to describe in detail the types of wounds he had treated as a MASH unit surgeon to paint a gruesome picture in the minds of the jurors.

Dr. Schaeffer responded, "Patients on our operating room tables received treatment for wounds sustained from multiple sources. Gunshot holes made from AK-47 ammunition, for example, or shrapnel from bombs perforating or tearing apart the victims' bodies. First, the surgical team identified any external wounds by clearing away obstructions including temporary bandages, clothing, and blood. Then, we took X-rays to locate objects that needed removal such as bullets and pieces of metal, to find sources of internal bleeding, and to identify any other complications such as bone fragments."

Fox said, "Thank you, Dr. Schaeffer. Would you describe for the jury Amy's condition and wounds when she arrived at the hospital?"

Dr. Schaeffer answered, "The paramedics were bagging her when she entered the trauma center because she was unable to breathe on her own, and—"

Fox jumped in: "Pardon my interruption, but what do you mean by 'bagging'?"

Dr. Schaeffer replied, "Bagging is when medical personnel—in this case the paramedics—squeeze a handheld apparatus, an inflatable bag attached to a mask, to force oxygen into the patient's lungs to keep her alive during transport to the hospital."

"Like this one?" Fox showed the jury the blood-stained resuscitator used by the paramedics when they had brought Amy to the hospital.

"Yes. Once in the trauma room, we intubated Amy, meaning we inserted a tube into her mouth and down her throat. The tube was attached to a machine called a respirator, which forced air down the tube, into her lungs.

"During our physical examination of Amy's body, we identified a hole in the side of her head where she had been struck by a pellet that penetrated the skull. The pellet had then traveled through brain tissue and exited the skull on the opposite side. Upon further observation, we found three round holes in her chest. The pellets had passed through the soft tissue of her lungs and exited her body out her back.

"At that point, I decided to move her to the operating room to perform the surgery necessary to repair the wounds. Once there, we inserted tubes through her chest and into her lungs to drain the fluids."

Fox asked, "Doctor, why was that so important?"

He replied, "The patient's blood pressure was falling because the fluids were restricting her ability to breathe and therefore maintain adequate levels of oxygen in the bloodstream to survive. Without the procedure, Amy would have drowned in her own blood.

"During the operation, we surgically repaired the internal damage caused by the pellets and the entry and exit holes. Then, we moved her to the intensive care unit for recovery and observation. The next morning my greatest concern was the injury to her brain, so I called Dr. Abraham Rabinowitz for a consultation. That afternoon, he examined Amy's brain injury, and we adjusted her medications. After that, her condition improved for several days until suddenly she was overcome by complications caused by her gunshot wounds. More specifically, a brain aneurism ended her life."

A somber mood captured the courtroom. Three jurors retrieved tissues from their purses. Even the judge paused to control the tears swelling in his eyes. He drank some water and said, "Let's take a fifteen-minute recess."

After the recess, Fox called his next witness. "Your Honor, the State calls Dr. Abraham Rabinowitz to the stand. Dr. Rabinowitz, please state your name and current position."

The doctor answered, "My name is Dr. Abraham Rabinowitz, and I am a credentialed neurosurgeon at Cornell University Medical Center, where I teach classes in the School of Medicine."

Fox replied, "Thank you, Doctor. You're being modest. Isn't it true Cornell University Medical Center is one of the leading neurosurgery centers in not just the United States, but the entire world? And isn't it true you are the doctor in charge of the neurosurgery department?"

"Yes, both of those statements are true," he said.

Fox resumed his questioning. "Please describe the results of your examination of Amy Colter."

Dr. Rabinowitz responded, "I assisted Dr. Schaeffer in the post operation evaluation and treatment of her head wounds. We were concerned she might be experiencing cerebral edema or swelling of the brain. Under normal conditions, we would have performed a verbal examination, but at the time, Amy was unconscious. So, we performed an observational examination and found no signs indicating that pressure was increasing inside the skull."

After Fox completed his questions for Dr. Rabinowitz, he called the coroner to the stand. "Mr. Wayne, did you perform the autopsy of Amy Colter?"

Wayne answered, "Yes, I did."

Fox presented various documents and asked, "Mr. Wayne, are these exhibits the forensics autopsy report, photos, and sketches of Amy Colter's body?"

He said, "Yes, they are."

Fox responded, "Thank you. Please read the highlighted sections of the report for the jury."

Coroner Wayne started reading and ended by confirming the cause of death had been a brain aneurism resulting from trauma sustained by multiple gunshot wounds.

Fox called his final witness, Linda Colter, and began, "Linda, I know these questions are difficult to answer, but the jury needs to share your experiences of that fateful day when the two defendants shot your daughter Amy.

"Your husband, Jack, is not in the courtroom today. The only information the jury will have to make their final decision with is the testimony and evidence presented in this trial. Would you please tell the jury why Jack is not in the courtroom today?"

Linda became emotional and answered, "My husband Jack is not here today because he died in Vietnam defending this county against evil men like them."

She pointed at Sal and Joey. Her stare pierced the air. "Jack is resting in Arlington National Cemetery in Washington, DC." Then, she jumped up and yelled, "But, if he were alive, your funerals would be next!"

The courtroom erupted. The jury was aghast.

Judge Newell slammed his gavel down and commanded, "Order in the court! Mrs. Colter. I know this is very upsetting, but we'll have none of that in my courtroom. Please try to control yourself!"

Fox paused to let the jury taste her rage then said, "Linda, could you tell the jury where you were when the shooting started?"

Linda replied, "I was in the kitchen making dinner when I heard gunshots outside followed by stuff flying through the air tearing the kitchen to pieces. I instinctively ducked down to avoid whatever it was. Then, I yelled downstairs to Amy's bedroom, 'Are you all right?' But there was no answer. That's when the fear for my daughter overwhelmed me."

Linda began to cry and stopped speaking as the painful memories of that day began to rise from the depths of their buried tombs. The jury listened empathetically. She gulped water from the glass on the edge of the witness stand and said, "I yelled again, 'Amy, Amy, are you all right?' I remember racing down the stairs and finding her lying on the floor. I was horrified. I don't remember anything after that."

Fox was already confident the State had proved Sal and Joey were guilty. But he knew their fate was sealed as he watched the jury's reaction to Linda's emotional testimony.

Chapter 12
The Verdict

Fox had purposely completed his prosecution late in the day to leave Linda's testimony lingering in the minds of the jury. The next morning, he rested the State's case, and Judge Newell announced, "Mr. Lautenberg, please call your first witness for the defense."

Lautenberg stood, "The defense calls Dr. Joseph Michaels to the stand."

Dr. Michaels was an expert on eyecare and taught at Yale University, one of the leading ophthalmology schools in the county. Lautenberg asked, "Dr. Michaels, how often should an individual like Mr. Carlson who is over sixty-five years old have an eye examination?"

Dr. Michaels responded, "Once a patient is sixty-five years old, we recommend an eye examination every year."

Lautenberg replied, "Why do medical professionals recommend an annual eye examination for elderly patients?"

Dr. Michaels answered, "Proteins in the eye for people over sixty-five start to break down, which can cause vision to blur or become cloudy. Humans have an amazing brain that can adapt to what we see. Sometimes, as vision fades as we get older, our minds adjust and trick us into thinking we can see fine when in reality, we don't see objects as clearly. That's why eye examinations should be performed at least annually on patients over sixty-five years old."

The defense team continued their procession of rebuttal witnesses, who tried to establish reasonable doubt in the minds of the jury. Lautenberg called Detective Miller to the stand.

"Detective Miller. Did you investigate the murder of Anthony Giancana?" Lautenberg asked.

Miller answered, "Yes, I did."

"Would you please tell the jury his relationship to Sal Provenzano?"

"Anthony was an assistant vice president of Teamsters Union. Sal was his friend and his boss."

"Detective, help me understand the timeline of events. Anthony was murdered just before the parked van was shot up outside of the Provenzanos' house. Is that correct?"

"Yes. That's correct."

"Now, Detective Miller. Did you investigate the murder of Joseph Salerno?"

"Yes, I did."

"And what was his relationship to Sal Provenzano?"

"They were good friends and played golf together every Thursday morning."

"Detective Miller. If two of your friends were recently murdered and a few days later, a suspicious-looking van was parked outside of your house for an exorbitant amount of time, would you be worried?"

"Yes, sir. I would."

At the conclusion of the questions for Miller, Lautenberg said, "Your Honor. The defense rests."

Judge Newell responded, "Thank you, Mr. Lautenberg. Closing arguments will begin tomorrow morning. This court is adjourned until nine o'clock in the morning."

The next morning, Fox stood in front of the brown railing surrounding the jury box and began by saying, "Ladies and gentlemen of the jury, Salvatore Provenzano and Joseph Provenzano are guilty of the charges of second-degree manslaughter. The State presented a preponderance of verbal testimony and physical evidence that proved beyond any doubt their reckless actions killed Amy Colter and her faithful dog Max. The defense wants you to believe the murder of Amy was an accident caused by poor judgment.

"Amy's death was not an accident. It was not because of poor judgment. Let's review the irrefutable facts. First, Sal and Joey willfully choose to load and reload their shotguns with powerful, tactical double-aught shotgun shells. Their intended purpose was to kill people in the van. You were horrified when you looked at pictures of the van torn apart by the destructive power of those shotgun shells. You examined pictures documenting the holes in the

Colters' house and immortalizing the mayhem in Amy's bedroom. That destruction was no accident.

"You listened in shock as Linda described the terror she felt as pellets soared by her head while she was making dinner in the kitchen. She screamed to Amy, 'Are you all right?'" He stopped and paused to let the jury hear the silent room, then added, "Did you hear that? That's what Linda heard. Only silence. Can you imagine the horror you would feel racing down the stairs into your child's bedroom? You saw pictures of the room. Can you see Amy and Max?" Fox paused again, as if gazing into the bedroom. He waited for each juror to visualize the scene.

Fox continued by saying, "Neighbor Henry Carlson, a war hero from Guadalcanal, provided eyewitness testimony that Sal and Joey repeatedly fired shotguns from the front window of the Provenzano house in the direction of the van parked in the street.

"Dr. Brewer, the leading forensic scientist in the United States, testified that tactical double-aught shotgun shells are used by the military and law enforcement personnel to kill their targets. Dr. Brewer further testified those powerful pellets penetrated the wall of the Colter house with enough force to kill Amy Colter while she was innocently playing in her bedroom. State experts testified those pellets caused Amy's death.

"Ladies and gentlemen of the jury, just a few miles from here stands the Statue of Liberty. Three of you sailed past her beacon of light on your way to Ellis Island when you entered the United States of America and applied for citizenship. The three of you became citizens because you wanted to live in a country with opportunity, but more importantly, in a country with freedom and justice for all. You wanted that not just for yourselves, but also your children."

Fox looked across the jury and asked, "Do you know what Lady Liberty is holding in her right hand? A book with the date of the Declaration of Independence in Roman numerals. The book is a law book that symbolizes justice and equality. Amy's father, war hero Jack Colter, is not here today. He is resting at Arlington Cemetery along with other brave men and women who died, who made the ultimate sacrifice defending freedom and justice. If Jack Colter walked through that courtroom door, stood where I am standing, looked you in the eyes ,and asked you this question, what would you say?"

Fox moved to the front row of the jury box and asked the first juror, "Mr. James Lee, will you vote for justice today and find my daughter's murderers guilty?"

He moved sideways and asked the second juror, "Mr. Robert Burton, will you vote for justice today and find the defendants guilty?"

Fox proceeded to ask the remaining ten members of the jury the same question.

When he finished, he said, "Your Honor, the State rests its case."

Attorney Lautenberg stood and approached the jury. "Good afternoon, ladies, and gentlemen. Thank you, Mr. Fox, for reviewing the evidence in this case, but you conveniently left out some key facts. Those facts provide more than a reasonable doubt that Sal and Joey were responsible for Amy Colter's accidental death. We all agree Amy's death was a terrible tragedy. As a society ruled by laws, you were asked as a jury to decide who was responsible. We want justice for Amy and punishment for the guilty. I want that just as much as you do. But you don't want to convict innocent neighbors, do you?

"Let's review the facts. First, the testimony of Mr. Carlson was not supported by another eyewitness. Mr. Carlson is a good man trying to do the right thing. He's a war hero who served our country in one of the greatest battles between good and evil in our county's history. But without a corroborating eyewitness, how do we really know who he saw in that window?

"Remember the testimony of Patrolmen Wagner and Connolly, who were two eyewitnesses at the scene of the shooting. They stated there was a cloud of smoke in front of the window of the Provenzanos' house. Is it possible the smoke obscured Mr. Carlson's vision?

"Mr. Carlson wears eyeglasses to help him see objects more than twenty-five yards away. The distance from his front porch to the Provenzanos' living room window was thirty-nine yards. Mr. Carlson is elderly now, and we all know the memories of people of his age aren't what they used to be.

"Here's what makes it even harder to find the truth. Dr. Michaels, the eye expert and professor at Yale, testified individuals over sixty-five years old should have an eye examination every year. Why is that? Remember, he said that over time, our vision starts to fade and objects can become harder to identify. Mr. Carlson is over sixty-five years old and admitted he has not had an eye examination for at least three years. Is it possible Mr. Carlson saw someone else in the window and just thought it was Sal and Joey because they live there?

"The next problem for Mr. Fox's fantasy story is that the police did not find any shotguns, empty shotgun shells, or double-aught ammunition at the Provenzanos' house. That means there was no physical evidence that proves Sal or Joey fired the shotguns that killed Amy."

Lautenberg continued with arguments and statements, adding fiction to raise more unanswered questions.

"In conclusion, the evidence presented during this trial raises more than a reasonable doubt that Sal and Joey committed a crime. We don't really know who did. Therefore, I ask you, the members of the jury, to find Salvatore and Joseph Provenzano innocent of the State's alleged charges. Thank you."

After the closing arguments, Judge Newell spoke to the jury. "Ladies and gentlemen of the jury, the evidence presented in this trial is for you to determine if Salvatore and Joseph Provenzano are innocent or guilty of the charge of manslaughter in the second degree. You will now be transported by bus to your hotel for deliberations and to make a decision. Take as much time as you need. When you reach a verdict, please ask your foreman to notify a member of your security team. After that, you'll be transported back to this courtroom."

At the hotel, the jury discussed the preponderance of evidence proving the accused were guilty as charged, and the foreman called for a vote. He was confident they would reach a unanimous verdict. But that was not what happened. Juror Barbara Ryan voted for acquittal on the first ballot, to the dismay of the other jurors. Then, she explained her reasoning. Hours passed as other jurors vehemently argued to persuade Barbara that Sal and Joey were guilty. Barbara held her ground.

On the second day, juror Mark Anderson unexpectedly changed his vote to not guilty. Heated arguments followed but to no avail. On the third day, the foreman notified Judge Newell that the jury was unable to reach a verdict. They were deadlocked and no amount of additional time would change anyone's vote.

Judge Newell was frustrated by the indecision of the jury to reach a unanimous verdict and summoned the twelve to the courthouse for questioning. US Marshals escorted the jurors one by one into his chambers, and he sternly asked, "Are you certain that with additional time and deliberations you will not reach a unanimous verdict? The heavily armed men standing behind you are US Marshals. They are here to protect you from any undue influence from outside this courtroom. Did anyone approach you and coerce you in anyway?"

Each juror said no. They had not been approached by anyone and confirmed more time would not change the outcome of their vote.

Judge Newell reentered the courtroom and declared that the court was in session. A hush encircled the gallery in anticipation of the verdict. Every seat in the courtroom was taken. The walls were lined with spectators.

Judge Newell thanked the jurors for their service then announced, "The jury is deadlocked and cannot reach a verdict. I am declaring a mistrial."

Sal and Joey celebrated their victory. The Genovese crime family's power and reach was too great for justice to prevail.

***

What the judge did not know was that Philip Castellano, the boss of the Genovese crime family, had decided to prevent the jury from convicting Sal and Joey of any crime. He had ordered one of his capos to get the witness list from one of their contacts in the Maplewood Police Department. Castellano had reviewed the list and picked a vulnerable juror to receive his instructions to vote for an acquittal.

Next, Castellano had ordered Capo Frank Gotti and his most ruthless soldier, Vito Costello, to deliver a message to juror Barbara Ryan. Barbara was a struggling single mother with two children. Her ex-husband, an alcoholic, had moved out of state to Pittsburgh, Pennsylvania, to avoid paying alimony and child support.

It was just another uneventful Saturday afternoon when Barbara parked her white Ford Fairlane in the driveway after returning from grocery shopping. She decided to check the mailbox, and halfway there, she heard a deep voice over her shoulder ask, "Barbara, how are you today?"

Barbara turned to see two large men wearing black overcoats and black fedora hats. Startled, she answered, "Who are you and how do you know my name?"

Frank answered, "That doesn't matter right now."

Barbara demanded, "What do you want?"

Frank replied, "Friends of ours need your help."

Barbara asked, "Who are these friends and what kind of help?"

Frank said, "You are one of the jurors in the Sal and Joey Provenzano trial."

Barbara was alarmed and said, "I can't talk about that. The judge gave us strict instructions not to talk to anyone."

Frank delivered Castellano's message: "We want you to vote not guilty for both Sal and Joey Provenzano."

Barbara objected, "I can't do that. Besides, the trial doesn't start until Monday. I haven't even heard any testimony or looked at any evidence. Why would I want to help your friends anyway?"

Frank decided to get to the point just as Vito's jacket opened up far enough to expose a large handgun in a brown leather holster hanging under his arm.

Frank reached into his pocket for a brown envelope and said, "We are reasonable people. We know you could use a little help yourself. We are willing to pay for your assistance." He handed her $5,000.

Nonchalantly, Vito chimed in, "Did you see on the news two weeks ago that a construction worker was thrown off of the fifty-sixth floor of a building in Manhattan?"

Barbara answered, "Yes. I saw the story on the news. What does that have to do with me?"

Vito replied sternly, "He didn't cooperate with one of our associates when he was asked to help a friend of ours."

Barbara was now scared and paused for a deep breath. She stared at Frank. *This guy looks like evil incarnate, but this other guy with the gun, he looks like a messenger from Satan himself.* His eyes were black as coal, and his face was disfigured by scars.

She watched ABC news every evening and knew the Mafia threatened, beat, and killed people with impunity. She realized her family was now in grave danger. The Mafia had no equal. No one could protect her or her family from the power and influence of the Genovese crime family.

Frank knew the money and gun would change Barbara's attitude to one of complete cooperation. For added encouragement, he said, "Barbara, how are your children Jerry and Claire doing in school? Do they like Jefferson Elementary? The driver of the yellow Carpenter school bus lives in apartment Number 112 on 327 South Prosper Street in Newark, New Jersey. Seventeen kids ride the bus every day with your two children. Would you like to have a guarantee Jerry and Claire will come home safely from school every day?"

Barbara grabbed the envelope and agreed to their demands. The alternative was terrifying. She loved Jerry and Claire so much. They were all she had in life. She would do whatever it took to keep them safe.

That was why on the first juror ballot, Barbara did not hesitate to vote not guilty. To mask her real reason, she argued the evidence presented by the defense had convinced her there was reasonable doubt that the Provenzanos killed Amy. The testimony of eyewitness Mr. Carlson was uncorroborated, and his vision was questionable. Her daughter was almost Amy's age and she empathized with Mrs. Colter, but the prosecution hadn't even found the shotguns.

During the first day of jury deliberations, Castellano decided to add an insurance policy to obtain an acquittal and discussed the eleven remaining jurors with Angelo. They mutually agreed juror Mark Anderson was the best choice, but first they needed detailed information about Anderson's wife and children. Castellano knew exactly where to get it. He dialed Lautenberg's number, and Anderson's file arrived two hours later.

Next, Castellano ordered Frank and Vito to persuade him to vote not guilty by threatening

Anderson's family. To do that, Frank needed the name of the hotel where the jury was sequestered. He dialed a police officer on his payroll, who told him that Judge Newell sequestered the jury at the Jefferson Hotel, located a few blocks from the Newark train station. Anderson's room number was 231.

As Castellano was reading Anderson's file, he pondered how to deliver a message without alerting the police protective detail positioned outside every juror's room. Frank had a solution. They could enlist the help of the maid cleaning Anderson's room. She could deliver Castellano's message in an envelope. No one would suspect her.

Frank and Vito went to the maid's apartment to solicit her participation in the clandestine scheme. She was a poor undocumented immigrant from El Salvador with no one to protect her from the threat of deportation—until now. Her cooperation was easy to obtain. She even smiled and said "Gracias" when Frank handed her five Ben Franklins.

Anderson returned to his room after the first day of deliberations and found an envelope on the nightstand. His curiosity changed to alarm after he opened it. He understood the message illustrated by the enclosed polaroid pictures. An evil-looking man was standing between his wife and daughter in front of their living room fireplace. He had draped his left arm across his wife's shoulder. The right arm was circled around his daughter's vulnerable white neck.

Anderson's knees buckled in terror when he looked closer. The man's right hand was holding an open-bladed barbershop razor. The enclosed note written on white hotel stationery read, "Contact the police, and your wife and daughter die. We have resources everywhere. Vote not guilty."

The anguish suffocated Anderson. His wife and daughter were more important than life itself. He would do anything to protect them. *The hell with justice*, he decided. He obeyed the message.

***

John sat stunned in disbelief when he heard Judge Newell announce the mistrial. He contemplated what to do next. The sight of Sal and Joey celebrating as they walked out of the courtroom doors as unpunished, free men enraged John. He thought, *These guys think they are untouchable just like the rest of the Mafia. Evil prevailed today in the battle for truth and justice. The good guys finished last.*

John knew the evidence presented at the trial was irrefutable and demanded a guilty verdict to balance the scales of justice. He asked himself, *What would Jack do if he were alive? Would he accept the verdict, turn the other cheek, and walk away? Or would Jack serve punishment with his own hands and kill them both?* The words *family*, *duty*, *honor*, and *country* resonated through John's mind as if Jack were shouting them from his grave at Arlington National Cemetery. Tears swelled in John's eyes. Then, his thoughts circled back to the Provenzanos.

This was not the first time the Mafia had gloated about defeating the justice system while leaving a courtroom in victory. The news media had even nicknamed one boss "The Teflon Don" after his sensational front-page trials ended in acquittals and the don stood on the courtroom steps bragging about his invincibility. The New York Mafia was flaunting their golden age of power. Why wouldn't they? Even the well-respected Roger Grimsby had announced on his evening ABC news broadcast, "New York was once called 'The Fun City,' but now it's called 'Fear City,' controlled by lawless men ruling every aspect of society through violence and murder."

John said to himself, *Not this time.* He was no longer a helpless child growing up in New Jersey living in fear of the Mafia. He was a formidable, grown man capable of exacting punishment on the guilty. John silently made a vow that at a time and place of his choosing, he would take the righteous sword from Lady Justice's hand and battle the Mafia's reign of evil. He would carry out justice for Amy and Linda in accordance with a higher moral law.

The evening after Judge Newell declared a mistrial, Castellano hosted a lavish party at his white seventeen-room mansion on Staten Island to celebrate the victory. He especially praised Frank and Vito for their efforts to persuade jurors Barbara Ryan and Mark Anderson to vote not guilty. In his closing remarks, Castellano bragged that the Genovese crime family was untouchable. *Who's going to stop us?* he thought. *We rule New York and have no equal.*

Father Time eventually served justice to Frank and Vito. Three years after the trial, the police found Vito Costello's decomposed body floating in the New Jersey Meadowlands. A shotgun blast had killed him instantly. A few years later, Frank Gotti died of cancer in the United States Medical Center for Federal Prisoners in Springfield, Missouri.

As for Sal and Joey, they returned to their criminal lifestyle in Murder, Inc. Sal re-established himself as the top-earning capo in the Genovese crime family. He had a renewed enthusiasm for violently killing anyone who dared oppose him. Joey climbed the leadership ranks by expanding into lucrative moneymaking ventures. The father and son duo lived life large in their world of greed governed by violence.

Sal's next big score involved stealing whiskey containers transported across the Atlantic Ocean from the Jameson distillery in Dublin, Ireland. He received a tip from a friend in the Teamsters that the whiskey was arriving at the Port Newark Container Terminal. When the cargo arrived, the longshoremen on the

Genovese payroll diverted ten of the orange whiskey containers onto trucks driven by Sal's men. Inspectors on the payroll waved the trucks right through the front gate to circumvent the internal controls that compared the container contents of the trucks with the terminal intake records. Office accounting personnel subsequently erased the shipping documents for the ten containers in the computer, thereby eliminating any record of their arrival in the United States.

Joey's first big moneymaking scheme also involved the Port of Newark. Joey used his father's contacts in the Longshoremen's Union to obtain details about lucrative incoming shipments. He soon learned a ship was arriving from Japan with containers filled with Sony Walkman cassette players. He knew they were worth their weight in gold and devised a plan to steal five trailer loads. After the trucks left the terminal destined for warehouses across the northeast, they were hijacked. The scheme netted Joey almost a million dollars after tribute payments to the boss, Castellano; the underboss, Galante; and his capo, Sal.

Joey was ambitious and continued to explore other avenues to generate piles of cash. His lust for power and prestige consumed him. He approached his dad with a new idea and suggested, "Why don't we diversify into legitimate real estate investments? I was skiing at Stratton Mountain Ski Resort last weekend and noticed the real estate market is booming. We could build and sell condominiums as a conduit to launder our cash."

Sal liked the proposal and said, "You find the land. We can use our friends in the construction business to build them. Find out what the building codes are and who does the inspections."

Joey replied, "That's the beauty of it all. I already checked with the Windham County clerk's office. There are no codes or building inspectors. It's out in a rural area of the mountains."

Sal was hooked.

Joey hired a local realtor to show him several parcels of land. Since he wanted to spend more time skiing, he also looked at a secluded log cabin house for a vacation home. He thought, *This property is perfect. We could even have Genovese retreats up here. We could sit in those Adirondack chairs on the porch, drink Scotch, and smoke cigars. And best of all, Stratton's population of two hundred twenty-three can't afford a police department. There're only three sheriff's deputies patrolling the whole county.*

When Joey returned, Sal gave his blessing to make the purchases. He especially liked the idea of using the log cabin as a base of operations in Vermont. Over time, the plan developed into a cash cow. Joey moved up the hierarchy and was rewarded with his own crew. Life was good.

Chapter 13
The War

After the trial, John's code compelled him to start a war against the Mafia to restore justice. He understood it was a dangerous idea and getting caught was not an option. He didn't want the Mafia to retaliate against him or his family. He knew an attack required careful planning and preparation, so he began by making a mental list of problems to solve.

The first step was to develop a plausible reason to go back to New Jersey without his family. He thought to himself, *Why not use the cover story of another hiking trip? It's the perfect alibi. I'll start at the Appalachian Trailhead at Springer Mountain, Georgia. In the meantime, I could use the next trip to Linda's as a fact finding mission.*

That evening at the dinner table, he discussed the possibility of the trip with Debbie and the kids. They agreed with excitement. Every time John returned from a wilderness adventure, his stories entertained them for weeks.

One of their favorite stories embellished a hiking trip that had occurred deep into the wilderness of the Grand Teton Mountains, just north of Jackson Hole, Wyoming. John had been in a remote area covered with dense forest when he noticed a mammoth grizzly bear crossing the trail forty yards ahead. The bear smelled John and stopped, stood up, and stared. John froze. He was paralyzed with fear but started taking deep breaths and exhaling slowly. He calmed himself long enough to surmise the predator's intentions.

He remembered friendly bears were relaxed, and their ears pointed toward the ground. Aggressive grizzly bears' ears pointed into the air after deciding to eat their prey.

The giant beast's ears were pointing straight into the air. John retrieved his Marlin 1895 Guide Rifle and chambered a high-powered 45-70 round. Just then, the bear charged. He fired the first round but missed, not compensating for the grizzly's remarkable speed. He reloaded. The second powerful bullet ripped into the bear's right shoulder. The angry bear was not thwarted and continued full speed toward John like a freight train barreling down the tracks. Time was running out. He chambered another round and adjusted his aim, then pulled the trigger. The ferocious grizzly fell dead inches from his hiking boots.

The Colter family had enjoyed delicious bear meat dinners for months, and the fur pelt became a comfortable living room rug.

The next problem John considered was how to get close enough to Sal without revealing his true intentions. *I know*, he thought. *In college, I was a member of the backstage crew in theater productions. We learned stealth-like techniques to enter the stage undetected by the audience.* He remembered hiding in the shadows wearing black clothing that cloaked his presence. *Yeah. I could do something like that to surprise Sal. We moved into the light for scene changes onstage and then vanished back into the darkness.*

He had also learned from a friend in the makeup crew how to use cosmetics and disguises to dramatically alter an actor's appearance. John decided to wear old, worn-out clothing and bought a dark-colored jacket and hat at the Goodwill store in Fort Scott.

With that problem solved, John thought to himself, *Now. What weapon should I use at close range? A handgun or maybe a knife.*

He remembered the day he was trained by an FBI instructor. John had been hauling hay on a sunny one hundred-two-degree summer day on Junior Voth's farm near Elk City, Kansas. Junior's brother Tim had been visiting from Quantico, Virginia, where he worked as an instructor for the FBI. On his visit, he had taught John to use all kinds of weapons.

John's mind scrolled through those memories, and he concluded a Smith & Wesson Model 19 revolver was the best choice. It had disadvantages: it only held six bullets, and it was slow to reload. But the advantages of accuracy and power at close range won the argument. He thought, *Where can I buy an untraceable revolver? I know.* He drove south to

Baxter Springs, Kansas, and purchased the gun at Raymond's Gun Shop using cash.

The plan was coming together. John started to feel good about its success. Then doubt leaned over his shoulder and asked him, *Do you really think you can escape the Mafia? They'll start a never-ending vendetta against you for killing a high-ranking member of the Genovese crime family. They will hunt you forever. Their tentacles reach everywhere, even out here in Kansas. If they find you, Debbie will be a widow.*

He vowed to plan for every contingency and minimize every possible risk. He knew he would never get caught if he carefully designed the attack, shooting, and escape. That's when John decided to create a diversion during the attack. *Let me think. What can I do to distract these guys? I know. I'll use a flash-bang grenade.* He remembered reading that the British Army developed the pyrotechnic grenades for the Special Air Service, the SAS, in the 1960s. It was designed as a non-lethal explosive device to stun intended victims without causing permanent damage. When the grenade exploded, it produced a flash of light and sonic wave that temporarily caused blindness, deafness, and disorientation.

He telephoned a specialty ammunitions supply store in Dallas, Texas, and asked about purchasing the device.

Colter's Code

The clerk replied, "Sure, mister. If you have enough money. But I'll warn you up front. You have to have a license and the federal government requires us to see some kind of personal identification document. We keep a ledger book of each purchaser's name and address. We usually use the buyer's driver's license."

John thanked the clerk and hung up. He knew that would provide a trail of evidence that could lead back to him. He thought, *Well, purchasing the grenade is not an option. What else can I do?* Then, he had an epiphany and smiled.

He purchased the chemical ingredients at multiple locations to render their origins impossible to trace. The main ingredients were magnesium and potassium nitrate, which, as it turned out, were so common that they were sold in farm supply stores all across the United States.

John's last problem to solve was where to stay in New York City without leaving a trail back to Kansas. He knew the perfect place to hide out before and after he completed the mission. The Brown's house on Staten Island. From there, he could ride a train to the other end of the line at St. George and then take the ferry across the Hudson River to Battery Park on the southern tip of Manhattan. It was located a block from the subway system and provided the perfect method of anonymous transportation through the underbelly of the city via its web of tunnels and train stations, allowing stealth-like access to the streets above.

Margret and Betty were two old spinsters who lived their lives in obscurity. Their only connection to John was their friendship with Grandpa Colter, and he had died many years ago. Margret was like a saint. She had sacrificed her dream of having a loving husband and children to become the primary caregiver for her young sister, Betty, after their parents died in a tragic car accident. Betty's genetic disorder caused physical and mental disabilities that limited her understanding of life to a childlike level.

Growing up, John had walked from his grandfather's house many times to visit them, and over the years they developed a lifelong bond. He never noticed Betty looked different than other adults or that she moved slowly and talked a little unconventionally. He only recognized her as part of the family.

For the next few months John kept planning for the mission. The calendar pages turned quickly, and soon the Kansas Colters arrived at Linda's. Once there, John began the process of observing Sal's patterns looking for an opportunity. He carefully watched Sal leave the house in the morning and return later that night. Then—*That's odd,* he thought one Thursday morning. *Sal never came home last night.* John made a mental note: *Find out where Sal stays on Wednesday nights.*

Colter's Code

On Monday, John drove to the Teamsters office and found Sal's Cadillac parked in front of the building. John situated his car a block down the street with a mirror viewing the Cadillac. He waited for Sal. Sal emerged an hour later accompanied by two large men, presumably bodyguards. They drove toward New York City.

John followed from a safe distance, hoping to go unnoticed by blending in with the other cars. It worked for a while until he lost sight of the Cadillac when the road funneled down from eight lanes into the two inbound lanes on the New Jersey side of the Holland Tunnel. John's car was pushed farther and farther away as each car waited its turn to enter. Sal's car was gone by the time John reached the New York exit. He returned to Linda's in failure. *Now what am I going to do?* he asked himself that evening.

Debbie, Linda, Lori, and Jack rode the train into New York City Wednesday afternoon to attend a family-friendly Broadway play. John had some free time and decided to use it to study Sal's habits. He wondered if Sal was so arrogant, he made the mistake of never changing his daily routines.

The afternoon hunt was unproductive. The dinner hour was approaching. John pondered, *Since I'm hungry, why not eat dinner at one of Sal's favorite restaurants? Sparks Restaurant is nearby. Maybe my luck will change.*

Mark E. Uhler

John walked into Sparks wearing a disguise he purchased on the way, sat at the bar, and said, "Crown Royal on the rocks please, with a splash of Diet Coke." He sipped his refreshing whisky. "Bartender," said John, "I've never been here before. What are you guys known for?"

He answered, "The shrimp cocktail is really popular for an appetizer. Our specialty is ribeye steak with mashed potatoes. It comes with our house salad."

"Sounds delicious. Thanks. I'll try the ribeye, medium. Oh, and I love shrimp. Let me start with that."

Sal walked through the door three minutes after seven escorted by a beautiful blonde. She was his mistress, the goombah. The two bodyguards followed. One stood by the door. The other sat in a barstool next to John and ordered an aperitivo.

John couldn't resist the temptation of a conversation, so he said with an Irish accent, "The guy you're with must be pretty important."

The bodyguard answered, "You don't sound like you're from around here."

John replied, "No, sir, I'm from Dublin, Ireland. Just on holiday visiting friends who live here in New York. They told me this place had the best steaks in town. Steaks in Ireland can't compare with your grain-fed American beef. When I'm here visiting, I love a good American steak."

The bodyguard responded, "Your friends told you right."

Without ordering, a large, rare T-bone steak arrived with a pile of mashed potatoes. The bodyguard devoured his meal.

John said, "Those mashed potatoes are to die for. Do you eat here often?"

Between mouthfuls the bodyguard mumbled, "Yeah. Every Wednesday. My boss loves the food here."

John had found the location he needed for his return date with Sal. In the meantime, John continued his conversation and ordered another Crown. Shortly thereafter, he paid the bill with cash. Then, he disappeared: no one noticed the elderly gray-haired gentleman exiting the restaurant.

Outside the restaurant, John scouted the street, studying potential areas to stalk his prey for the attack and the surrounding neighborhood for avenues of escape. Before long, he found a hiding place: there was a spot between two tall buildings that created an invisible location in the shadows. He also discovered two dark alleys with dumpsters where he could change clothes and dispose of his disguise after the ambush.

He looked up and down the street and decided the best way to escape was the subway. There were three train stations in different directions, each within a reasonable walking distance.

Chapter 14
The Money

While John was traveling back to Kansas after he shot Sal, the phone rang back at the Colter residence.

"Hi, Debbie, is John there? This is Andy," the voice said.

Debbie answered, "Hi, Andy. He's not here right now, but he should be back tomorrow. He's driving back from one of those hiking adventures of his, this time the Appalachian Trail down in Georgia. Thank you again for attending Amy's funeral. We really appreciated you coming."

Andy replied, "Well, in a way, that's why I'm calling. Sal Provenzano was killed yesterday outside of Sparks Restaurant in New York City. I thought you and John would want to hear the news right away."

Debbie sighed with relief and said, "I'm glad he finally got what he deserved. Do the police have any suspects?"

"No. The assailant used some kind of explosive device to stun Sal's bodyguards, and then he shot him. When they regained their senses, the bodyguards searched the neighborhood, but the shooter just disappeared into the night."

After Debbie hung up the phone, she asked herself, *Was John really hiking in Georgia? He lives by a righteous code founded on a strong belief system and was very upset that Sal was not punished. He confidently told me after the not-guilty verdict Sal and*

Joey would receive justice someday. I don't think this was a random coincidence. Maybe I should ask him when he gets home? But do I really want to know the answer?

A few weeks later, John was teaching one of his economics classes at Pittsburg State University when a student asked him a personal question. At the beginning of every class, John encouraged his students to ask questions about topics other than economics because he believed it was an opportunity to motivate them to investigate those subjects outside of the classroom.

The student asked him, "Why did you choose to stay in Pittsburg all these years? You grew up in a suburb of New York City, one of the greatest cities in the world. There's Broadway plays, the Metropolitan Museum of Art, the symphony, and world-class professional sports, not to mention the amazing restaurants. It's also the financial capital of the world, with endless opportunities for fame and fortune. You gave up all that to live in a small town in the middle of America."

"Well, it pretty simple, really," John said. "My life is based on a code of character and values. What's important to me is my family and friends, not money and power. I love my wife, Debbie, and we decided to stay in Pittsburg to live close to her family and our friends. That's where I find the greatest joy in life."

"How did you two meet?" one of the girls asked.

"We met on a blind date at a fraternity dance here in Pittsburg. A mutual friend Brenda Johnson, who was a senior at the time at PHS, was dating my fraternity brother Scott Braun. She thought we were the perfect match. The dance sparked an attraction, and we started dating. And then it happened at her high school senior prom." He smiled as he reminisced.

"She was wearing this stunning yellow evening gown. The band started playing a slow love song, and I looked into her sparkling big brown eyes as her alluring black hair was brushing against my shoulder. Cupid's arrow pierced my heart."

John paused as he thought, *I'm thankful for Debbie every day. She's my strength and encourages me to be the best man I can be.*

Another student said, "But you did become rich as the result of your invention, and some would say powerful because of your political and corporate contacts."

"Well, I didn't plan it that way. It was the result of a confluence of events. It began one day when I was a young boy swimming with my best friend, Jimmy, at the Jersey Shore on Long Beach Island. A shark attacked Jimmy, and the emerald-green water changed to dark red. I yelled for help as I pulled his bitten body to safety. Jimmy's haunting screams inspired me to start a quest to find out what attracted the shark. He survived but I kept wondering why had it mauled Jimmy?

"The next summer, I was vacationing with my uncle on Cape Cod, Massachusetts, and he took me to the Woods Hole Oceanographic Institute. During the tour, I learned that marine biologists had discovered sharks were repelled by the electrical signature waves emanating from larger marine life. That experience rekindled my curiosity to find out why sharks attacked humans. A few years later, I invented a small, waterproof, battery-powered device capable of sending continuous electrical impulses through saltwater to repel sharks. The underwater trial tests simulated various human swimming conditions that might attract sharks such as wearing flashy jewelry, murky water with limited visibility, splashing to create loud noises, and blood in the water. The sharks swam straight at the test subjects, including children, and then at twenty feet, the sharks turned around and disappeared. After that, I started that manufacturing company here in Pittsburg. Sales exploded and profits soared, and, as they say, the rest is history."

A student in the front row said, "Some people say you're a self-made man. How do you answer that?"

"No one is a self-made man. My mother taught me to live a life with character and to tell the truth. She encouraged me and told me I could accomplish anything in life: first I had to believe in myself, and then I had to try. On the farm, Junior Voth taught me so many valuable lessons about hard work, perseverance, and unconditional love for family. I watched my mentor John Cardullo interact with other professionals and learned to patiently discuss opposing ideas with respect and conviction. I could go on with a list of so many people who cared enough to encourage me and teach me. The journey along the road of life is difficult. No one navigates the treacherous twists and turns without the help of others."

"What about your father? Didn't he help you become the man you are today?" the student asked.

John paused before he answered, "Not in the way you would think. After he abandoned me and my brother to live with my mentally ill mother when I was fifteen, I decided that for the rest of my life, my mission was to be the opposite of my father. For example, he never told us he loved us or gave us positive reinforcement like giving us a hug and encouraging us. I tell Debbie and my children I love them every day and always give them a big hug."

A last student asked, "How did you end up teaching at the same university you attended years ago as a student?"

John answered, "That's a good question. After we accumulated substantial wealth, Debbie and I decided to pursue new dreams and adventures. I always wanted to be involved in teaching, and she encouraged me to obtain a PhD in economics. So, we moved to Austin, and I enrolled at the University of Texas."

After class, John experienced an introspective moment and wondered, *If these students knew that I killed Sal Provenzano, how would they judge their professor? Would they consider me a hero, villain, murderer, or righteous executioner? But what about justice? Who balances the scales of justice when the criminal justice system is corrupted by the guilty?*

That spring, the Kansas Colters traveled to attend the Larsen family reunion held at the Nansen Lodge of the Sons of Norway on Staten Island. The day was filled with fun games, laughter, family stories, delicious Norwegian delicacies, and plenty of cold beer, especially Pabst Blue Ribbon and Schaefer. This year, the loss of Amy brought a sad, gray cloud to an otherwise bright sunny day.

John was sitting on a picnic bench drinking a Pabst and talking to his older cousin Eric Larsen when he discovered a new opportunity to attack the Mafia. Eric started reminiscing about the good ol' days and suddenly said how much he missed sweet little Amy. "I'm glad that mob guy finally got what he deserved," Eric said.

The word "mob" triggered a question, but first John downed another cold one.

"Hey, Eric, last year at the family Christmas party, you mentioned the Mafia was involved in the construction industry in New York City."

Eric answered, "Yeah, they sell every yard of concrete poured at the construction sites for all the building projects in the city."

John was curious and asked, "How do you know that?"

"Well, my best friend Gary Allen is an estimator for TRH Construction Enterprises. They're one of the biggest general contractors in the New York City area. Turns out that TRH Construction is building the Trump Tower over on Fifth Avenue and Gary's the estimator reviewing the bids. You've heard of Trump. He's that famous rich guy who puts his name on all his buildings and stuff.

"Anyway, one night, Gary and I meet at Paddy Doyle's Irish Pub after work for drinks. We're pounding down pints of Guinness and then start drinking Irish car bombs. You remember what a car bomb is? It's the drink where you drop a shot of Jameson into a pint of Guinness. Then you chug it without stopping, all in one breath.

"So, Gary and I get hammered. Then he starts talking about confidential work stuff because he's drunk. Stuff he's not supposed to tell anybody. Gary tells me he's reviewing this concrete bid for the Trump Tower, and he notices a line with no description at the bottom. It's for ten percent of the total concrete bid. It's millions of dollars. He calls the concrete salesman and asks the guy, 'What's the ten percent for?' The concrete salesman says it's the share that goes to the mob. He says to Gary, 'Think of it as the Mafia's tax for doing business in New York City.'"

John replied, "Why doesn't someone report the extortion payments to the authorities like the building inspectors or New York Police Department?"

Eric laughed. "John, you have a lot to learn about the dark side of New York City. The building inspectors and police are on the mob's payroll. Let me tell you a real-life story. I'm at work one day at the construction site, and this guy gets so pissed off at the foreman, he yells, 'I am going to report all you fuckers to the police. That's right. I am going to tell them about all the corruption on this job.'

"Well, the next day, we come back to work and there's the mouthy guy propped up against the construction entrance wall for everyone to see entering the job site. The dead guy's wearing a sign that reads, 'RAT.' Haven't you watched the movie *The Godfather*? Threatening or standing up against the Mafia is no joke."

The story rekindled John's resolve for justice against the Mafia. He had an idea. *Why not strike a direct blow to the Mafia's source of power: the money.*

The Mafia was collecting millions of dollars from this concrete extortion scheme. Then, they used some of that cash to bribe corrupt law enforcement officials and the building inspectors to protect the scheme. They used the rest to pay for their lavish lifestyles.

John realized disrupting the flow of cash from the illicit concrete extortion payments was an opportunity to inflict substantial financial pain. He surmised that the concrete company received a paper check for payment of concrete delivered to each job site. Then, the company would deposit those checks at their bank and write another check to the Mafia. That paper trail was evidence. John wanted copies of those checks.

He knew banks were required by federal law to maintain confidential records of every bank deposit and check for five years. Once a bank paid a check, it was microfilmed and the paper originals were temporarily stored in check filling machines. Then, they were mailed monthly to the customer along with the bank statement and deposits. He wondered, *How can I get copies of those checks? Banks have sophisticated security systems and other systems to protect the confidentiality of every customer.*

He discovered the answer a few days after the picnic. The Colter family rode the train into Manhattan for some sightseeing. Jack and Lori wanted to visit FAO Schwartz to marvel at the wonderland of stuffed animals, toys, and games. As they walked up Fifth

Avenue, John noticed a line of concrete trucks at the Trump Tower with "Lombardo Concrete: Bayonne, New Jersey" painted on the side.

The following day, John went to the Maplewood library and located the section of printed phone books. He found the Bayonne phone book and searched the yellow pages for Lombardo's phone number and street address. Then, he flipped to the list of banks, thinking that Lombardo would have his checking account at the closest bank for convenience. *That's interesting. The address of Union National Bank is three blocks down the street from Lombardo.*

Later, John called the Lombardo number.

A woman answered, "Hello, this is Lombardo Concrete; may I help you?"

John replied, "Yes. I hope so. This is Adam Reynolds with AM Morris marketing. We're conducting a customer service survey for Union National Bank just down the street. Is there someone who could answer a few brief questions? The bank is interested in improving their customer service to small businesses in the area."

She said, "Well, Mr. Lombardo handles all the business with the bank. We've done business with Union for years. He's out right now. Can I take a message?"

John didn't want to leave a phone number that would trace back to him.

He answered, "That would be great. But I have to call a lot of other customers, and I am afraid my line would be busy. I'd be happy to call him when he comes back. What would be a good time?"

She replied, "He should be back after three."

John ended the call by saying, "Thank you so much for your help. Have a good day."

John's mind envisioned a workable plan, but one hurdle remained: how to get inside the bank to access the check storage machine without getting caught.

He decided to case the bank to get some idea on how to get the checks. The opportunity came Thursday night. John exited the Metro bus a few blocks from the bank, and as he walked past the front windows, he noticed a janitorial crew cleaning the lobby. The lights were on, and it was as bright as the day inside. He reasoned that meant the alarms would be turned off, so he went down the alley behind the bank for more reconnaissance. He couldn't believe what he saw next. The cleaning crew had propped the back door open, presumably to carry trash to the dumpster. He seized the moment and entered through the back door.

Once inside, he found the check storage machine in the bookkeeping department. He paused and looked around. *Good, no one saw me.* He flipped a switch, and the machine's trays started rolling. The janitorial crew's vacuum cleaners' noise muffled the sound of the machine's vibration. He stopped at the letter L and thumbed through the names. There it was: Lombardo Concrete Company. He grabbed the bank statement full of checks and deposits and stuffed them in his pocket.

Suddenly, someone yelled, "Hey, you. What the hell do you think you're doing in here?"

Startled, John turn to see one of the janitors standing in a doorway holding a big black trash bag.

John answered, "I saw the back door was open and needed to pee really bad, so I came in looking for a bathroom."

The man eyed him suspiciously. "What did you take from that machine?"

"Why, nothing. Nothing at all," he said, backing away toward the opposite doorway.

The man retorted, "I don't believe you. I saw you put something in your pocket." His voice grew louder. "Put it back!"

John kept inching closer toward the exit door.

The man commanded, "Stop right there!" John bolted out of the room hearing, "I said stop. I'm going to call the police."

The police department dispatched a patrol car to investigate an intruder at the Union National Bank. The patrolmen interviewed the cleaning crew and gleaned little tangible information to identify the tall man. They drove their squad car around the neighborhood but found no one matching John's description.

No one noticed the missing bank statement until two days later when the bookkeeping clerk found Lombardo's slot empty.

A week later, Jerry Freling, special agent assigned to the Federal Bureau of Investigation office in Newark, New Jersey, received an envelope from Union National Bank. He read the typed note, "From a Concerned Employee." The enclosed bank statement had paid checks and deposits for the Lombardo Concrete Company. Five checks for one million dollars each were payable to the five New York Mafia crime family bosses. Within days, the FBI installed secret wiretaps on the Lombardo Concrete Company telephones. Information obtained from the listening devices justified wiretaps on every concrete company doing business in New York City.

The investigation mushroomed and exposed an intricate web of corruption. Over the next two years, the government indicted and convicted over one hundred mobsters and corrupt government officials. The five families were furious that the flow of tens of millions of dollars of extortion payments was eradicated.

After the week at Linda's, the Kansas Colters returned home to their daily lives at work, school, and the children's extracurricular activities such as league sports and music lessons. John knew that the summer break from school was the next opportunity to attack the Mafia and began planning the next installment payment of pain as further retribution.

One evening at the dinner table, Debbie, John, and the kids discussed when they should go on a hiking adventure together. John suggested they hike part of the Appalachian Trail in Vermont the next time they visited Linda because it was only a few hundred miles north of Maplewood. The trail had beautiful scenery, mild elevation changes, cool temperatures, and plenty of water.

Summer arrived, and the family traveled to Vermont to escape the sweltering Kansas heat, where daytime temperatures were already approaching one hundred degrees. Debbie, Jack, and Lori were excited to share the wilderness experience with John. They especially enjoyed the sounds of the birds and the wind whistling though the treetops.

At midday, as they were hiking up Stratton Mountain, they found a mountain stream, John filled Lori's water bottle, and he dropped in two pills. After thirty minutes the pills dissolved, and the water was almost ready to drink. He didn't tell Lori the pills were necessary to kill the bacteria and microorganisms like tiny giardia parasites. Next, he showed them how to filter out the dirt and other visible particles like pieces of bark and leaves.

Lori was so thirsty she started chugging the water, then stopped and spit out a mouthful. Her face cringed and she said, "That's disgusting. I can't drink that." Moments later she added, "Mommy, I think I'm going to throw up."

John realized it was a teaching opportunity for the family to learn a critical survival skill and said, "If you want to join me on hiking adventures in the outback, you have to do unpleasant things and drink water like that to survive. Your body needs at least a gallon of water a day and each gallon weighs eight pounds. You can't carry all the water you need, so you have to find water sources like this one."

Chapter 15
The Robberies

On the first Monday in Maplewood, the seeds were planted for the next opportunity to strike a blow against the Genovese crime syndicate. Debbie and Linda brought Jack and Lori into the city for a fun afternoon in Central Park to explore the Ramble and the Lake, eat a picnic in a meadow, and walk along the lush pathways. Dinner reservations were at seven thirty, so John had plenty of time to find the next location to attack.

Previously, John had written an article called "The Mafia's Origins and Rise to Power in the United States" for publication in the quarterly bulletin of the Federal Reserve Bank of Kansas City. In the article, John concluded enormous amounts of illicit cash were generated from alcohol sales during Prohibition. Mafia leaders had then used that cash as seed money to exponentially expand their criminal activities.

As part of his research, John had read a report from the FBI office in New York detailing how the mob collected extortion payments in the Fulton's Fish Market area of Downtown Manhattan. After the couriers collected the payments, they delivered the cash to the "bank" in the back room of the Blind Dog Bar on Water Street. The cash was held there for safekeeping and transferred once a week to an impenetrable location.

Mark E. Uhler

John found a coffee shop on Water Street with a window view of the Blind Dog Bar. He watched and sipped his coffee while munching down a pastrami sandwich on rye with mustard and read a *New York Times* newspaper. Then, he wondered, *What prevents a courier with sticky fingers from stealing money along the route? There must be some kind of cash control besides the threat of cutting off your hand or worse. A written ledger, perhaps, listing a set payment amount that the bookkeeper compares to the cash received in the envelope.*

John watched the couriers arrive one by one, then walked around the neighborhood to find an unassuming location to change appearances. He entered the Blind Dog Bar dressed like a tourist wearing sunglasses, a nondescript collared black shirt, and South Street Seaport hat. As he sat down, he said hello to the bartender and ordered a Schaefer lager on tap. Sipping the beer, he gathered information about the layout of the room. The back door opened briefly, exposing the gateway to the bank. He caught a glimpse of two big men inside, a desk stacked with a pile of cash on the top, and an older man sitting behind it.

John finished the beer then paid for the tab with cash, adding a generous tip. At seven thirty, he joined the family for a memorable dinner at Tavern on the Green.

Colter's Code

On Thursday, John returned to Water Street to rob one of the couriers who was collecting cash payments for the Genovese crime family. He was easy to identify. He was wearing the same clothes and clutching the brown handbag full of cash. John discreetly followed the courier, watching him during the next few collection stops.

John's pace accelerated to launch the attack. He placed his left hand on the boy's right shoulder and commanded him to stop. The courier turned in surprise, thinking, *Who the hell is this guy?* John was towering over him, wearing a wig, white t-shirt, sunglasses, and a New York Yankees baseball hat. He pressed a gun barrel into the courier's ribcage and pushed him into an alley.

The kid snarled, "You're making a big mistake, old man. Do you know whose money this is?"

John answered, "Yes, I do. Now hand me that bag. Your life can't be replaced; dead is forever. It's not your cash anyway."

The kid knew the cardinal sin of a courier's life was giving the cash bag to anyone except the designated Genovese banker. His mind started racing with thoughts of the painful consequences of arriving at the Blind Dog Bar emptyhanded. His fear swelled to terror until resolve propelled him to action. The courier's eyes gave away his intensions.

The kid jabbed his right elbow into John's side. He feared the Genovese family more than the imminent threat. Then, he hit John with a weak left jab and thought to himself, *The fight is on, old man. I'll take you down.* He would defend himself against this villain and robber. He would be the hero who saved the day. His mind envisioned the reward for his courage.

John anticipated the left punch after the elbow's blow. The unathletic boy stood five feet, six inches tall, and weighed one hundred forty-two pounds soaking wet. He was no match for a six-two, two hundred forty-pound skilled fighter.

The Genovese family recruited couriers based on honesty and loyalty. They relied on the powerful threat of retribution as the deterrent for any potential robbery against one of their "protected" couriers.

The impact of the boy's blow barely phased John. He slid the nine-millimeter Glock pistol into his belt. Then, he swiftly landed a right jab on the side of the boy's jaw. The powerful force knocked him down onto the sidewalk. He was stunned long enough for John to grab the brown bag and start running to make a clean getaway.

The resilient courier rose from the concrete and chased his mugger down the sidewalk just in time to witness the guy jump into a yellow cab. Alertly, he memorized the cab number. With no time to waste, the boy ran as fast as he could to the Blind Dog Bar.

A Genovese soldier guarding the bank immediately noticed the rattled courier didn't have the brown bag. The side of his face looked like a hammer had hit him. The banker sitting in his chair counting the pile of cash quizzically said, "What the hell happened to you? Where's the bag with all the money?"

The courier gulped for air and panted, "I don't have it. Some old man just robbed me a few blocks from here. I ran here as fast as I could to tell you."

The banker stood up and said, "Take a few more deep breaths and tell me exactly what happened."

The kid answered, "I was walking down Water Street making my pickups when this old guy grabs my shoulder. Then he shoves a gun in my ribs and tells me to give him the bag. I say to the guy, 'No way, don't you know you're stealing from mob?' Then, I decide to stop the old dud and hit him in the chest with my elbow. The next thing I see is this big fist hitting me in the face and knocking me down on the sidewalk."

The banker asked, "Then what'd you do?"

The boy said, "Well, he wrestled the bag away from me and ran away, so I got up and chased him. Around the corner, he jumped into a cab. Here's the cab number: two, five, six, seven. That's the last time I saw him."

The banker called the Genovese headquarters in Greenwich Village.

A stern voice answered.

The banker asked, "Is Donnie there?" Donnie Martinelli was the capo of the crew operating in that section of town.

The man answered, "No, he's out."

The banker replied in frustration, "Well, let me speak to Angelo. It's urgent."

Angelo came to the phone and asked the bookkeeper, "What's so urgent?"

He answered, "One of our couriers just got robbed at gunpoint a few blocks from the Blind Dog Bar."

In irritation, Angelo said, "What do you mean, a courier got robbed? Who the hell is stupid enough to rob us? Where is this courier?"

The banker replied, "He's right here. He said he chased the man that attacked him, but the guy escaped in a yellow cab. He got the cab number."

Angelo asked, "What'd this guy look like?"

"It was some old guy wearing sunglasses and a Yankees hat," the banker said.

Angelo responded, "I'll be right there."

Angelo was furious. On the drive over to the bar, he mumbled to himself, *Nobody robs us and gets away with it. I'm going to find this guy and torture the hell out of him while he begs and begs me to stop. Then, I'm going to cut him up into little pieces and feed him to the fuckin' fishes.*

Angelo burst through the Blind Dog's door like a raging bull. He was accompanied by four intimidating soldiers armed with sawed-off shotguns. He barked at the banker, "Where's that kid?"

The banker pointed and said, "He's sitting right over there."

Angelo walked over to the courier and demanded, "Have you ever seen that guy before?"

The boy was holding an ice pack on the side of his face and in submission, replied, "No, sir, never."

Angelo said, "Describe this old guy to me."

The boy retold the story and added, "He was a lot taller than me. I'd guess maybe over six feet." Then, he demonstrated how he'd hit his attacker with his elbow. Angelo realized that the diminutive kid's elbow wouldn't have been effective against a grown man. He thought to himself, *At least the kid has the guts to try and stop this guy.*

Angelo hollered over to six-foot-four Eddie Hudson, one of the soldiers, "Come over here. Is the guy this tall?"

The boy responded, "He's tall like him but bigger and stockier. Now that I think about it, the guy might have worn some kind of a disguise. He sure was athletic for an old guy. The way he hit me and the way he ran. When he jumped into that cab, it sure wasn't like how my grampa moves."

Mark E. Uhler

Angelo asked the bookkeeper for the cab number. He paused and wondered, *There are too many similarities between this guy and Sal's killer to be coincidental. Was this the same guy?* He had a lead and would find out.

Angelo dialed the telephone number of the Yellow Cab Company.

A man answered and Angelo said, "This is Angelo Galante."

The man recognized who Angelo was and listened intently.

Angelo commanded, "Call the driver of cab number two, five, six, seven, and tell him to get over to the Blind Dog Bar right away. I need to ask him about a rider he picked up about an hour ago."

Peter Clayton arrived at the bar soon after the cab company radio dispatch operator told him to report immediately to Angelo at the Blind Dog Bar. A personal invitation to a bar operated by the Genovese crime syndicate was a serious matter. Clayton took a deep breath, nervously walked inside, and said, "Hi, I am Peter Clayton, a cab driver for Yellow Cab Company. Is Angelo here?"

The shotgun-toting soldier replied, "He's in the back. Go through that door."

The sight of Angelo terrified Clayton. His demonic eyes and chiseled face resembled a stone-cold killer's. The intimidating soldiers holding big, scary guns added to the tension in the room. Clayton said, "Sir, you wanted to see me."

Angelo answered, "Yes. I need your help and want you to answer some questions for me." Before Clayton could respond with, "Yes, sir, anything you need," Angelo continued with, "You know who we are and what we do? You picked up a guy on the corner of Water and Pine about an hour ago. Tell me what he looked like."

Clayton responded, "Well, I picked up what I originally thought was an old white guy wearing a plain white t-shirt. He took off his sunglasses and hat, and I noticed in the mirror his eyes and forehead didn't look that old. His shirt was tight, making him look really muscular, like he played football for the New York Giants or something. He grabbed a cloth like a handkerchief from a pocket and wiped stuff off of his cheeks, like makeup. Then he didn't look so old. Maybe he was thirty to forty—"

Angelo interrupted, "Where did you drop him off?"

Clayton answered, "I dropped him off in front of the Wall Street subway station on Broadway."

Angelo asked, "Did he leave anything in the back seat?"

Clayton replied, "No, sir. He gave me a twenty-dollar bill for a five-dollar fare and said keep the change."

That gave Angelo an idea. Maybe there was a usable fingerprint on that twenty-dollar bill? If there was, his contacts in law enforcement would find him. The tangible lead aroused his hunting instincts. Then, he asked, "Do you have that twenty-dollar bill?"

Clayton said, "Yes, sir." He pulled it out of his pocket and handed it to Angelo.

Angelo grabbed the corner, walked to the table, and carefully placed the bill in an envelope. Then he called the police station and said, "Is Detective Brunson there?"

A minute later he answered, "Brunson here. What can I help you with?"

Angelo replied, "This is Angelo. Come to the Blind Dog Bar right away. I have a job for you."

Brunson quickly responded, "I'll be right over."

When he arrived, Angelo handed Detective Brunson the envelope.

He asked, "What's this for?"

Angelo answered, "Enclosed is a twenty-dollar bill. Run the bill for prints and see if you can find out who this guy is. Then report back to me immediately."

The following day, the homeless shelter in the Bowery received a brown bag with $609 in cash wrapped in rubber bands with a note that read, "Food for the hungry."

John returned to the Blind Dog Bar two weeks later to extract the next installment payment in his war against the Genovese crime family. This time, he was there to rob the whole bank. He altered his appearance again and walked into the bar dressed in a blue pinstriped suit and a red tie. To add to the ruse, he dyed his hair blonde and wore nonprescription eyeglasses. The loose-fitting suit jacket concealed the nine-millimeter Glock handgun holstered under his left arm.

John sipped a Schaefer and ordered a cheeseburger with French fries. He wanted to appear like one of the lunch crowd of hungry professionals. As the minutes passed, the patrons paid their tabs and trickled out the front door, leaving the bar almost empty.

It was time. John used his napkin to wipe his fingerprints off of the beer glass, plate edges, and silverware, then asked the bartender, "Where's the men's bathroom?"

He casually strolled toward the bathroom and paused beside the door leading into the bank. John turned slightly with his back to the bar, replaced his eyeglasses with a pair of dark sunglasses, and pushed earplugs into his ears. Next, he opened the door and tossed in a flash-bang grenade, slamming it shut before the projectile hit the floor.

The explosion rocked the door, and he reopened it to confirm the intended results. The room's occupants were stumbling around holding their eyes and shaking their heads from the concussion effect of the blast. He removed the sunglasses and earplugs, withdrew the Glock pistol from his holster, and entered the room. Seconds later, his duffel bag was full of cash. Before he bolted for the door, he looked down and noticed a ledger book. The cash didn't object to its extra company in the duffel bag.

The three remaining businessmen sitting at the bar turned to watch the events unfolding like it was a Hollywood movie, except this was real. They watched the patron in the blue pinstriped suit emerge from the back room with a large bag hanging over his shoulder. He was holding a gun in his right hand. A puff of gray smoke meandered through the door.

Suddenly, John's eyes registered a flash behind the bar. He heard a loud bang followed by a pop as the bullet penetrated the brown paneled wall behind his left ear. There, he found the source. The bartender stood across the countertop aiming a revolver toward John. Thankfully, the bullet had missed. John aimed his Glock and fired. The round was true and propelled the bartender into the row of liquor bottles behind him. His body ricocheted onto the old wooden floor as broken glass, bottles, and alcohol rained down to join him.

At first, the three barstool onlookers curiously watched the gunfight. Then, they dove to the floor for safety when John aimed his pistol toward them. They posed no threat. He didn't fire.

John ran toward the front door to escape. On the way, he glanced across the bar to find the bartender. There he was, lying on the floor with bright-red blood oozing out of a hole in the center of his chest.

John was an expert marksman who didn't miss his target at that distance. He practiced firing his weapon religiously, and the bartender made the inexperienced mistake of hesitating before firing a second time. John didn't give the dead man a second chance.

He expected the guards would regain their senses at any moment and enter the room with their guns blazing. He was right. He paused and instinctively looked back in search of any threats, just in time to see an angry soldier wielding a sawed-off shotgun step through the cash room door. John fired two consecutive rounds, propelling the guard backward.

John ran out the front door and down the street. As the front door closed, two guards emerged from the bank in time to see him. They raced after him out the door, knocking a lady down as she walked her dog on the sidewalk.

They looked in every direction. "There he is!" one proclaimed. The chase was on.

John zigzagged around some pedestrians as he ran down Water Street and turned at the next corner. He was hoping his pursuers wouldn't notice and slowed down to blend into the crowd. *Are those guys still chasing me?* he wondered as he looked back.

The two soldiers, wielding their pistols in broad daylight, rounded the corner. They were in hot pursuit and gaining ground.

John darted across the street, weaving around the moving cars, and then turned down an alley. The guards weren't as nimble. One bounced off the hood of a slow-moving Chevrolet Impala but recovered and picked up his pistol, then hobbled toward the alley. The other had to stop or get run over by a speeding taxicab.

John soon realized he had made a critical mistake leaving the crowded street where the pedestrians shielded him from the soldier's bullets. In the alley, John was an easy target. The only cover was a dumpster. He sprinted toward it and was startled by the blast of a gunshot. The bullet ricocheted off the brick wall. The guard's heart was pounding so hard from the chase, he couldn't accurately aim the iron sight at the end of the barrel. The shooter inhaled a deep breath to calm down and confidently pulled the trigger. The bullet burrowed into the bag of cash, sending what looked like a puff of confetti into the air.

John turned to return fire but hesitated when he saw someone walking on the sidewalk behind the gunman. He didn't want to shoot an innocent pedestrian by a mistake. District Attorney Fox had told him Amy was collateral damage. John's code stopped him from pulling the trigger.

That pause gave the soldier time to regain his composure, and he pulled the trigger. This time, the bullet traveled true to the target.

The red-hot missile pierced John's right thigh, sending a bolt of pain throughout his body.

The ensuing battle was like the gunfight at the OK Corral in Dodge City. A cloud of gunpowder smoke filled the alleyway like a morning fog. The air smelled like rotten eggs.

John overcame the excruciating pain in his leg and returned fire in rapid succession until the clip was empty. Blood trickled down his leg and pooled inside his sneaker. Two bullets hit one of the Mafia gunmen. The other ducked back around the corner as bullets whistled through the air. He looked over at his partner lying in front of the alley. Blood was squirting intermittently out of his neck. His eyes were staring at the sky. Then, he convulsed and stopped breathing.

The survivor yelled into the alley, "I'm going to get you. You motherfucker."

The warning gave John time to duck behind the dumpster and reload another clip.

The angry guard emptied his six-shot revolver at the dumpster and lurched back.

John stepped back into the alleyway, fired two rounds, and ducked behind the dumpster.

The guard heard the bullets whiz by his head, then he returned fire.

Six more bangs followed by silence. John knew the guard was reloading. He looked across the alley and noticed a door. He limped over, stood halfway through it, and fired two rounds for suppressing fire, then slammed the door.

The kitchen staff froze as they watched John hobble past them wielding a large handgun and exit into the main dining room. The pain in his leg stabbed him with every step. He grabbed someone's brown coat hanging from one of the oval leather booths' wooden pole hooks and limped out the front door.

The coat's owner yelled in disbelief, "Hey, man, that's my coat!"

Then the patrons witnessed a second man burst through the kitchen door flashing another large handgun as he intently searched for the man with the limp.

He shouted, "Where's the guy who just came through here?"

A frightened woman sheepishly pointed toward the front door.

Outside, the gunman became frustrated. He didn't see John. Dejected, he looked down at the sidewalk and noticed red droplets. He followed the trail down the sidewalk, but they started to dissipate. Then, he stopped and looked dismayed. The red drops had completely disappeared.

After John went out the door, he spotted a Metro subway sign and dragged his throbbing leg toward the green railing at the entrance. He stepped onto the escalator's silver stairs and went down. He knew at the bottom the deep maze of turns and hallways provided multiple directions for escape. On the first platform, he looked down at the tracks. No approaching train. He needed a train to get away.

He looked again into the dark tunnel for an oncoming beam of light and listened for the sound of screeching wheels pressing against the steel rails. Nothing. He couldn't wait. He feared the guard would find his target again.

John hopped down into the track area, sending another lightning bolt of pain into his wounded leg. Now he was committed. He limped to the opposite platform, carefully avoiding the third rail that carried the deadly six hundred twenty-five volts of electricity powering the trains. Halfway there, he moved faster as he heard the squealing sound of steel wheels getting louder. He made it. Then, he pressed himself up onto the platform. The waiting passengers watched aghast. The train slowed. The doors opened. He boarded just as the gunman arrived at the opposite platform and helplessly watched.

John couldn't help himself and waved goodbye. The gunman flipped him his middle finger.

After a few stops, he exited the subway system in Harlem wearing his belt tightly wrapped around the bullet wound. Down the street he found a pharmacy.

The clerk noticed the limp and the belt covering a reddish-brown stain streaking down the outside of John's pants and said, "What the hell happened to you, man?"

John answered, "Some guy tried to mug me a few blocks from here. He demanded that I give him my duffel bag and I told him to get lost. Then he pulled a switchblade on me. When he lunged, I blocked the knife, and I punched him right in the face, knocking him down onto one knee. That's when he stabbed my leg and got up and ran away."

The clerk asked, "Hey man, you want me to call the police?"

John replied, "They aren't going to do anything."

"Yeah. The guy's long gone by now, anyway. We have a bathroom in the back if you want to bandage that up."

In the bathroom, John dropped his pants and looked at the hole in his leg. He knew he needed surgery and called Jan Stevenson, his mother's old friend from childhood. She was an operating room nurse at Mount Sinai Hospital.

She answered, "Hello. This is Jan."

John replied, "Hi, Jan. This is John Colter. I need your help. Do you still live in Hoboken?"

***

Jan examined John's leg and said, "You really should go to the hospital."

He understood but insisted that was not an option. This had to be off the books. She reluctantly removed the bullet, sutured the hole closed, and dressed the wound.

During the procedure, Jan glanced down at the large duffel bag and said, "John, I don't know what you got yourself into, but I …"

John stopped her before she could ask anything else and said, "Jan. You've known me a long time. All I will tell you is what I did was for a good cause."

The *New York Times* headline the next day read, "Cheeseburger Bandit Robs the Blind Dog Bar." The article reported that during the robbery, the bartender and a guard were shot to death attempting to stop the perpetrator. Another guard was also shot to death during a chase down an alleyway. The bar's owner did not disclose the amount of cash stolen.

The police department knew the assailant was shot by a security guard and contacted area hospitals to find their gunshot victim. Emergency room personnel reported they had no intakes matching the killer's description.

Back at their Greenwich Village headquarters, Castellano was infuriated when he heard how much cash was stolen, but the loss of the ledger book also caused considerable distress. The book contained the name of each business making the extortion payments, the amount of each cash payment, and the dates paid.

Castellano barked, "Who is this guy and how do we find him? I want that book back and I want this guy dead."

Angelo answered, "Boss. The guy is like a ghost. Every time he hits us, he's wearing some kind of disguise and manages to disappear. The police have some nine-millimeter bullet shell casings from the robbery, but without a gun to match them to, that's pretty much a dead end. This guy's pretty smart. The police crime lab technician at the scene said the guy was eating greasy French fries and that they should have found fingerprints on his glass, or fork, or something. But the guy wiped everything clean."

Castellano yelled in frustration, "Who the hell does this guy think he is? When we get him, I'm going to dump his tortured body on the street in front of Blind Dog Bar to send a message: don't fuck with the Genovese family."

Angelo said, "This guy's probably ex-military and had Special Forces training. He's just too calm under pressure to be a civilian. His elite skill level with a handgun takes years of practice."

Castellano said, "Maybe this guy is working for the government. I'll contact our friends and ask them to investigate if there's any possibility the hit on Sal and robbery at the bar were part of some kind of vendetta against us." Then he paused and added, "I know just the right guy to ask. I'll call Eddie Warren at the CIA. He'll know if the government was involved.

"I collaborated with him during World War II when the Allies invaded Sicily. He was the guy in the United States government who asked us for help before the American Army landed on the beaches. We contacted our family back in Sicily to solicit their power and influence to weaken the Italian Army's resistance when the Americans landed. The word went out from the Sicilian Mafia: 'If you fight against the Americans, you'll answer to us.' The Mafia's threat to kill them and their whole families was so effective, many Italian soldiers didn't even go to the battlefields, or if they did, they didn't fire a shot. General Patton's army charged across the island with only weak resistance. Our efforts to help the CIA and the United States government saved a lot of American lives. The secret deal with the CIA never became public, and the CIA kept its promise all these years to continue our mutually beneficial relationship. Warren still calls us once in a while for help, and we call him with special requests."

The Bowery Homeless Shelter in Downtown Manhattan received an anonymous cash donation a day later in a duffel bag. The $191,000 was the largest donation the shelter had ever received. The note read, "Food for the Poor."

The staff was curious who the donor was when they found a .38 caliber bullet inside the bag and some bills with bullet holes but were thankful for the gift.

John returned to Linda's that evening with a noticeable limp. Debbie knew something was wrong and she asked, "What happened to your leg?"

John answered, "We need to have a talk, but let's wait until the kids are asleep."

Debbie agreed, recognizing the disturbed look on John's face meant this was going to be a serious discussion.

John sat beside her on the living room couch holding her hand and told her the truth. The code prevented him from lying to her. Debbie's intuition had given her suspicions already from too many coincidences. She hadn't had the desire to ask him, but now she knew. She leaned over and hugged John, silently rejoicing in the knowledge John had killed Sal Provenzano as justice for Amy.

Then she said with a sly smile, "So. You gave the money to a homeless shelter near Little Italy in the Bowery. Nice touch. Are you finished, or is there more you need to do?"

John answered in a questioning tone, "I'm not done yet. Is there any reason I should stop now?"

Debbie replied, "John, I you know you well enough to know whatever you do, you'll plan it carefully and finish what you start." She kissed him and with teary eyes added, "Just be careful. I love you."

Two days later, Detective Brunson called Angelo to report the results of the fingerprint search from the twenty-dollar bill retrieved from the cab driver. The police lab did find two usable quality prints. Unfortunately, they didn't find a match on the fingerprint index cards in New York or New Jersey. Brunson expanded the search nationally using the FBI's database and the military personnel files warehoused at the National Archives Records Administration in St. Louis, Missouri. Still, no match.

Brunson also told Angelo that the explosive device had been made using chemical ingredients that were too common to trace. They believed it was made by an expert chemist because the slightest mistake would have ignited the chemicals and blown up the maker.

Chapter 16
The Senator

The wheels of justice for Amy's killers had turned toward righteous punishment with the death of Sal. But the scales remained unbalanced. The weight of the Genovese crime family's evil empire was overwhelming.

District Attorney Fox had suspected jury tampering and discussed the possibility with Judge Newell after the trial. The judge agreed something didn't smell right. He thought the body language of Barbara Ryan during the trial had been very suspicious. He was shocked and dismayed that the jury had not rendered a unanimous guilty verdict. He knew the evidence was irrefutable and wondered why they had not convicted Sal and Joey of their crimes. So, Newell personally conducted unprecedented posttrial interviews of each jury member. He wanted to ferret out the truth and ask if anyone had approached them to change their vote. He even asked federal marshals to explicitly offer each juror witness protection.

It was odd that jurors Anderson and Ryan didn't ask any questions, and the judge sensed their minds were preoccupied. But he didn't know how Castellano had got to them.

Anderson and Ryan had decided justice was a noble, intangible idea, but the death of a loved family member was reality. They knew any violation of Castellano's instructions guaranteed punishment with extreme violence. He demanded absolute obedience and silence.

The judge contacted the FBI to request that they investigate the possibility of jury tampering and obstruction of justice. But they found nothing out of the ordinary. A few months later, the FBI ended their investigation in frustration.

John was also suspicious and went to Fox's office to ask him for his opinion. Fox knew Castellano had a history of jury tampering, which had resulted in other mistrials. He explained to John that he had discussed the possibility with the judge: they suspected someone got to two jury members, but they couldn't prove it. Then, Fox looked at John and said, "Off the record. We suspect Philip Castellano, the boss of the Genovese crime syndicate, secretly used his people to get them to vote not guilty."

John was a businessman and university professor. He knew the person at the top of every organization ultimately made the final decisions. In this case, Castellano had to have approved the jury tampering. John decided to exact his own retribution. He thought, *If the United States government can't stop this guy, I will. I need to know more about Castellano, and I know who to ask.*

Kansas Senator Roscoe Turner answered the call.

John asked for a meeting and then arranged a business trip to Washington, DC. As a cover story, he told everyone the purpose of the trip was to discuss economic development and job creation in Southeast Kansas.

The clandestine meeting was held at the Mayflower Hotel. John sat in a red leather chair drinking a Macallan 18 and gazing out the window across Connecticut Avenue. Senator Turner approached and said, "John, how are you? I hope that file from FBI Director Kelley was helpful. Amy's loss was a terrible tragedy. She always had that contagious smile. I'm sure it's really tough on her mother, Linda. First, she lost her husband in Vietnam, and now Amy."

John replied, "Thank you, Roscoe. Amy always remembered the day you took her to visit Jack in Arlington and held her tiny little hand and told her that her daddy was a war hero."

After a few more pleasantries, the conversation turned serious when Roscoe said, "As I mentioned the last time we spoke, the Senate Judiciary Committee is investigating the activities of organized crime throughout the United States, especially the five New York Mafia families. And when I told Chairman Bond that Amy was a friend of mine and two mobsters in the Genovese crime organization had killed her and then walked free, the shit hit the fan. He said he was sick and tired of the Mafia not getting punished for their

Colter's Code

crimes. He got so mad he said he was going to call Attorney General John Bailey and order him to get the Southern District of New York office off their lazy asses and use the RICO statutes to take them all down. We passed those in 1970 to give law enforcement the tools to win the war against organized crime. We called it RICO because 'the Racketeer Influenced and Corrupt Organizations Act' was a mouthful. The law basically makes it a federal crime to operate an enterprise through a pattern of racketeering activities."

Roscoe paused to take a sip of his Scotch. "So far, they haven't done a goddamn thing to use the new law. But they will now." He took another sip and said, "After he met with Bailey, Chairman Bond sent the lawyer, Cornell University Law Professor Robert Blakely, who wrote the law for the Judiciary Committee, to New York for a week to teach them how to use the RICO statutes to prosecute the Mafia's leaders. Hopefully, that will light a fire under the DA's office and get some results. Some hotshot United States Attorney named Rudy Lancaster was just getting started on a major investigation.

"It didn't end there. The chairman subpoenaed Director Kelley of the FBI to testify. He wanted to know how a travesty of justice like that could have happened. During the hearing, he asked the director what the FBI investigation had discovered. The FBI suspected Philip Castellano had given the orders to tamper with the jury to obstruct justice. But so far, they didn't have sufficient evidence for a formal indictment—"

John interrupted, "That's why I asked for this meeting. What can you tell me about Philip Castellano?"

"Well. I don't know much." He paused to think. "I'll get you a copy of his FBI file like I did for Provenzano. By the way, did you know Sal Provenzano was killed a while back?"

John answered, "Yes. I understand that he was shot in front of Sparks Restaurant. Was it some kind of mob hit?" He wondered, *Should I tell Roscoe it was me? I think I can trust him. After all, he did get me that information on Sal.*

While John was talking, Roscoe looked into his eyes and noticed something different. He knew from John's confidence that somehow; he had been involved. He had known John for years, and John was instrumental in fundraising for Roscoe's campaign for the senate. John personally had given a sizable donation. He wondered, *What is John up to? I don't know, maybe I should ask him. But whatever it is, I'll keep helping him with whatever he needs, without question.*

Then the senator smiled and said, "John, let's have lunch more often. We could discuss what projects you're working on in New York City and what kind of help you need." He didn't have to wink for John to get the subtext.

John replied, "I'd like that. I do need help occasionally on these special projects."

The senator ended the meeting by saying, "John. Remember. Fortune favors the bold."

John returned to Kansas and waited for the FBI file. In the meantime, he started his own investigation into Castellano. Fox had told him Castellano was a very public figure and liked lots of attention. "He is always in the news," Fox had said.

John thought, *I'll start at the university library. They have copies of the* New York Times *newspapers going back two years.* There, he started perusing the headlines and pictures of stories related to Castellano's activities. After that source was exhausted, he searched the older copies archived on microfiche using a special machine to magnify and view the articles. As he read more and more, John thought to himself, *Fox was right. Unlike the other Mafia dons, Castellano loves the spotlight. There are plenty of articles describing his activities.*

John's favorite article was about Castellano's seventeen-room white mansion on Benedict Road on Staten Island. The picture showed it surrounded by an intimidating eight-foot-high brick wall. The black iron front gate was epic. The news media called it "The

White House" since it resembled the president's residence in Washington, DC.

The FBI file arrived in a plain manila envelope, with no return address. With it, John had hit the mother lode and now had enough detailed information to formulate his attack plan. But it would have to wait: the next window of opportunity wasn't until the semester break over the Christmas holidays.

The thoughts of Christmas rekindled some of John's favorite memories as a child before his father abandoned the family. Then he remembered one gift in particular that had provided a lesson that changed his life.

***

Christmas morning had arrived. John euphorically sprang from his bed ready to find the brightly colored packages Santa had nestled under the tree. He grabbed Jack, and they ran down the hallway in exuberant anticipation. Down the stairs they flew to discover Santa's packages of joy. John grabbed the largest one with his name on it. It was encased in green wrapping paper and had a white bow. He tore off the paper, and a picture revealed the box's contents. It was a radio. He was so excited, a big smile engulfed his face. It was the dream gift he had written at the top of his Christmas wish list.

He opened the box. *Wait, what's this? This isn't a radio.* He was staring into a Heathkit box full of wires,

Colter's Code

transistors, resistors, and various other kinds of parts that he needed to build his own radio. Moments later, his brother shared the same experience when he opened a larger package containing a Heathkit to build a combination radio transmitter/receiver.

Their father, who was one of the electrical engineers who had designed the first Telstar weather satellites, wanted to teach his boys an object lesson: that if you work hard and persevere, you can accomplish anything.

Jack and John looked at each other with skepticism. Exasperated, John said, "Why couldn't we get a radio that was already put together like other kids?"

The two brothers spent the following weeks in the basement reading the complex instructions and assembling the parts to construct working radios. As part of the process, they had to bind the transistors, resistors, and other components together by soldering the parts onto a circuit board. Solder was made from lead and melted at an extremely high temperature by touching the solder to the red-hot tip of an iron tool called a soldering iron. The tip liquefied the lead to bind the parts and wires together when the solder cooled down.

The project taught the boys a valuable lesson, and they gained self-confidence that they could fix or build anything if they committed and persevered through failures and hardships.

The process taught John another valuable lesson: you will pay a painful price for the lack of focus.

John was talking to his brother and not paying attention. He reached for the soldering iron, and instead of grabbing the insulated safe handle, he grabbed the burning red-hot tip of iron. The excruciating pain rocketed through his fingers. Reacting without thinking, he jerked his hand away, but no relief. The iron had burned so much flesh, it was attached to John's hand.

Quick-thinking Jack came to the rescue. He grabbed the insulated handle and yanked it off. They stared in horror, looking at the charred flesh and exposed finger bones.

While the boys had been disappointed on that Christmas they did not receive assembled radios, the lessons learned surfaced in many chapters of their lives. Jack became a highly decorated Army Ranger, completing one of the toughest training courses in human experience. John endured failure after failure, but by believing in himself and through perseverance and a you-can-do-it attitude, he invented a shark repellent device that saved the lives of people around the world. It also gave millions of people the confidence to swim in the ocean without the fear of a shark attack.

Chapter 17
The Park Bench

The Kansas Colters arrived the week before Christmas. Linda's spirit leaped with joy. Debbie looked around the undecorated house on the first morning and announced, "Who wants to go to the country in search of a Christmas tree?" It was the first Christmas without Amy. Linda had been too depressed to climb the attic stairs and bring down bright decorations to fill the house with cheer.

They piled into Linda's white Oldsmobile Cutlass, and off they went. The Christmas tree farm wasn't far, and after a brisk walk, Lori shouted from the last row of trees, "How about this one, Aunt Linda?"

Jack cut down the white spruce with his uncle's old bow saw, the one with the worn red handle. It had cut down many Colter Christmas trees.

Once they arrived home, the decorating party began, and the house filled with the aroma of cookies baking in the kitchen. Lori and Jack helped use the cutting molds to make sugar cookies in the shapes of stars, Christmas trees, and Santa Clauses.

The once-lonely living room sprang to life like summer lilies.

A day later, John drove everyone to the Chart House in Weehawken to share a holiday family dinner. The New York City skyline across the Hudson was spectacular. They marveled at the illuminated silhouettes of the tall skyscrapers outlined against the dark winter sky. It was like the buildings rose from the depths of the Hudson River to try and touch the clouds. During dinner, John walked by the crowded bar of thirsty patrons to the men's restroom. On the way, he noticed three men sitting on a hallway couch. His eyes caught movement. The serious man in the middle was handing a large brown envelope to one of the other well-dressed men. John glanced at his face. He couldn't believe who was sitting right there. It was Joey Provenzano. He was talking so intently he never noticed the tall man walking by. Later, John noticed Joey surrounded by a group of men at the bar and thought to himself, *I wonder if Joey comes here very often. I'll have to find out.*

The next morning, Debbie and Linda drove the kids to the Short Hills Mall for their annual Christmas shopping excursion. Part of the tradition was a festive lunch at the Altman's Department Store restaurant. John wasn't invited because the kids wanted to shop for his gifts, so he seized the opportunity to drive down memory lane on Staten Island. He had his own traditions. He drove to the Larsen homestead in Eltingville where his mother was raised. Grandpa Larsen had built the two-story house with his own hands shortly after he arrived as a penniless immigrant from Norway.

He parked the car to reminisce, and a tear swelled in his eye at the sight of the white flagpole. It was still there. Grampa had carved it from a raw, tall, straight pine. Snow began to fall, rekindling many fond Christmas memories. He visualized uncle Fynn juggling dulles, those special round Norwegian pastry balls Grandma made every Christmas. He remembered eating sugar-coated *krumkake* cookies, similar to crispy thin waffle cones, and watching his cousins joyfully opening colorfully wrapped presents.

On the return drive, John detoured past Philip Castellano's palatial white house to perform reconnaissance of the security. The walls appeared as intimidating in person as in the newspaper article picture. The entire perimeter telegraphed a message to keep out and not mess with the owner. Four guard buildings punctuated the message. They looked like turrets guarding a medieval castle.

John decided an attack on Castellano inside that fortress was futile. He might make it in, but he sure would never make it out alive. He thought, *I'd better wait and find a failsafe location. Patience is a virtue. I'll serve justice to Castellano somewhere else. It's more important that I promised Debbie I wouldn't get caught.*

The next day, John visited Fox to go fishing for more clues.

Fox welcomed John by saying, "Mr. Colter, come in. How are you today?"

John replied, "I'm well, sir. Thank you for allowing me to come by and ask some questions about the status of the investigations into Castellano for jury tampering and obstruction of justice."

Fox answered, "Of course, anytime. As I told you during our last meeting, I'm sincerely sorry about Amy and our inability to bring her killers to justice. Did you know someone killed Sal Provenzano a few months ago outside of a restaurant in the city?"

John answered, "Yes, I did know that. Wasn't it right in front of his mistress and two bodyguards? I guess, his life's choices finally caught up to him. Do the police have any suspects?"

Fox responded, "No, not that I know of. Sal's killer just vanished like a ghost into the belly of the city. Word in law enforcement was the two bodyguards protecting Provenzano that night 'got disappeared.' The police speculate they were executed and then buried somewhere."

John circled back to the original question: "Is there anything new about Castellano?"

Fox answered, "The FBI investigation remains open, but at this point, they have no evidence they can use in court. Every time they generate a lead, they hit a brick wall. It's totally out of control. Law enforcement and the justice system are almost powerless to stop them. For example: we suspect Castellano personally murdered over a dozen people.

And we believe he makes the decisions and gives the orders to orchestrate a large criminal enterprise. The problem is we can't assemble enough evidence for an indictment because witnesses don't remember anything, or if they do, they later recant their stories. Other times, the evidence just conveniently disappears from the police station evidence locker rooms, and the case falls apart. When we do get enough evidence to go to trial, the jury gets corrupted. In the end, the Mafia always wins. There is no justice or punishment."

John looked out the window toward Sparks Restaurant in New York City and thought, *Justice emerged from the darkness and met Sal on that sidewalk. Castellano's next, but where and how?*

Then he said, "I read in the newspaper that Castellano lives in a seventeen-room mansion on Staten Island. I drove by it the other day, and it looks like one of the Rockefeller estates. How can he afford a house and acreage like that?"

Fox replied, "He rules the most powerful Mafia family in New York. His illicit activities generate millions of dollars from extortion, prostitution, drugs, and gambling. And then there's cash-cow industries like concrete, garbage disposal, hotels, and restaurants. Oh yeah. There're also unions like the Longshoremen and Teamsters."

Bearing down on his reason for coming to Fox, John said, "You mentioned concrete companies. Isn't there a big concrete company on Staten Island? I remember driving by one when I was a kid visiting my grandfather."

Fox answered, "You probably drove by the DeLuna Concrete Company. That's one we traced to Castellano. We have surveillance photographs of Castellano driving from his house to the concrete company in the morning. From there, he goes to his office in Greenwich Village in the afternoon. When he's done, his bodyguard drives him to his apartment at Thirty-Sixth Street and Park Avenue. On weekends, he stays at the mansion. I got to tell you, he loves driving around in his flashy black Cadillac Fleetwood." John remembered the car from the FBI file Roscoe had sent him.

"That's interesting." John paused and said, "Well, I've taken up enough of your time. Thank you for the update. My family appreciates everything you did for us during the trial, especially your kindness to Linda. We'll always be grateful for all your help."

Fox responded, "Good to see you again, John. Let me know if I can help anytime in the future."

Fox had just given John the information he needed. Every day, Castellano drove from Greenwich Village to his apartment on Park Avenue. *There's got to be somewhere along that route I can get him. I'll check it out.*

The next day, John proceeded to drive along Castellano's daily route to select the best location for the attack. It wasn't hard to find multiple locations to hide and wait for the black Cadillac Fleetwood.

But the holiday season ended without an opportunity for John to takeout Castellano, and the Colters said goodbye to Linda at Newark Airport with hugs and kisses. Back home, John had time to think about Castellano and develop a plan. First, he needed a reason to return to New York City alone.

The NCAA March Madness basketball tournament gave him the opportunity. The University of Kansas men's basketball team was playing in the regional final at the Meadowlands Arena in East Rutherford, New Jersey. They were John's favorite college basketball team, and the arena was ten miles west of New York City. Perfect!

Luck smiled on John when the North brothers, his basketball-loving friends, called and invited him to go. They had four tickets and one had John's name on it. What could Debbie say? The Norths were like family.

John knew he needed to change tactics to confuse the Mafia after killing Sal and the robberies. So for Castellano, he would wear a different disguise for his attack and another to mask his escape. This time, he would dress like a homeless person. That way, he would blend into the local scenery—and it would be easy to conceal a weapon and wear a getaway disguise underneath the jacket. Vagrants lived all over New York on city streets, in parks, and at their favorite place: the warm underground subway hallways. He would look just like one of them.

Next, he asked himself, *What kind of weapon should I use? In Sal's case, I used a Smith & Wesson revolver, but it only holds six bullets and was cumbersome to reload. This time, I'll use a Barretta nine-millimeter like I did during the robberies. It was a good choice. I'd be dead in that alley without the extra bullets and ability to reload with the push of a button.*

The Norths booked the airlines tickets from Kansas City to Newark, and they were on their way. The East Regional basketball games started on Thursday afternoon with the year's Cinderella team, Richmond, losing by two points at the buzzer to the top-ranked Syracuse Orangemen. In the second game, Kansas crushed local favorite Seton Hall by a score of ninety-five to sixty-seven. John and the North brothers were excited because their Jayhawks had advanced to Saturday's final game. But their dreams of Kansas winning the national championship were dashed when the Orangemen prevailed and sent the defeated Jayhawks team back to Lawrence. The disappointed Norths flew home Sunday morning without John. He told the Norths he had some unfinished business to attend to in the city.

That afternoon, John caught a cab to the Staten Island Ferry Terminal to spend a few days at the Browns. It was the perfect hideout and part of the subterfuge to remain in the New York area.

On Monday, John started reconnaissance of Castellano's daily travel routine beginning in Greenwich Village. There, he discovered a restaurant across the street from the Genovese headquarters. He sat and waited for Castellano. The food wasn't great, but the meal filled his belly. The Cadillac Fleetwood arrived after three in the afternoon. The driver parked in front and waited for his boss. Within an hour, two large bodyguards stepped out of the entryway, looked around the neighborhood, and signaled Castellano it was safe to advance to the Fleetwood.

John considered returning the next day to shoot Castellano exiting the building, but decided it was too risky. The only escape route was down a long street that would expose him to deadly gunfire.

John patiently watched the Fleetwood disappear around a corner. He thought to himself, *I'll have to find a location somewhere else along the route. Maybe a temporary bottleneck where traffic slows to a standstill or better yet, a route where traffic is completely gridlocked at a red light.*

He continued his search for a possible location but wasn't satisfied and reentered the subway station at Thirty-Third and Park for the return trip to the Browns.

Mark E. Uhler

He paused by the turnstile to study the subway map of the streets and avenues and reconsider the most probable route from Genovese headquarters to Castellano's apartment. He traced the colored overlay of each rail line with his finger and found the nearest subway station. *Well. Looks like the best way is to drive east on Houston Street, then turn north on Lafayette. That turns into Park Avenue.*

Then, the seeds of doubt and discouragement entered John's mind as he realized the number of possible routes. *There're too many ways he could go. He may not even go to the apartment tomorrow. I only have two days to get this right.* As he studied the map, he had a eureka moment. He retraced one of the possible pathways. *This is it.* At the intersection of Fifteenth Street and Park Avenue, he found a city park called Union Square. He jumped on the next subway train and exited two short stops later.

John circled Union Square and found a park bench located on the corner of Fifteenth Street. He thought to himself, *This bench is the perfect place to wait. It has a clear view of the traffic at the light.* Then, he noticed that when the traffic light changed, the traffic was jammed together bumper to bumper. The stream of pedestrians meandering though the crosswalk slowed the traffic even further as the people and vehicles jockeyed for a passageway to navigate the congested intersection.

This is the place. He had a good feeling about it.

John entered a nearby pizza restaurant the next evening for dinner wearing blue jeans, black Nike sneakers, an "I Love New York" sweatshirt, nonprescription eyeglasses, and a New York Yankees hat. He was holding a Macy's shopping bag to add to his ruse. It worked. He looked like just another clueless tourist sightseeing in New York City. Inside the bag he had hidden a change of clothes purchased at an out-of-town Goodwill store. John munched down two slices of pepperoni pizza and went to the bathroom. There, he changed clothing and added makeup. Just after seven, a homeless man exited the restaurant.

Mr. Homeless had crooked fake teeth and scruffy black hair that was partially covered by an old dingy hat. He was wearing a dirty raincoat that smelled putrid. To add to the performance, he walked with a slight limp. John had always wanted to be an actor.

He deposited the Macy's bag in a trash cylinder. A street vender gave him a cup of coffee to warm his poor, destitute soul. A green park bench was his new home.

Time passed slowly. He asked pedestrians if they could spare some change. His filthy fingers protruded out of holes torn through his old gloves. The empty coffee cup he held began to fill up with coins. He patiently sat, watching the oncoming cars for his target to arrive.

Finally, there it was. Castellano's Fleetwood crept closer then stopped. It had to wait for the traffic light to turn green. John stood and ambled toward the crosswalk. Behind him, the traffic light changed to green, but the Fleetwood froze to avoid hitting the stopped car in front of it. The light turned red, and a sea of pedestrians swelled in front of the motionless line of vehicles.

John's heart was pounding from the adrenaline rushing through his veins, and his mind perceived the imminent dangers. He visualized the attack unfolding and sauntered toward the limousine, carefully watching the chauffeur for any change in behavior indicating he recognized the approaching threat. John passed the driver's door and stopped next to the passenger door window. He paused and thought, *After shooting Castellano, the driver will try to exit the car. He has to turn at an awkward angle before he can fire his gun at me. That will give me enough time to eliminate him last.*

John inhaled, pulled out the Barretta, flipped off the safety, and fired two high-velocity hollow-points rounds. The tinted window shattered. Castellano was sitting in the back seat. He was shocked and exposed. Another man was sitting beside him. The next two hollow points ended Castellano's life. Two more ripped through the other man's chest as he attempted to pull a handgun out of his holster.

Just as John anticipated, the chauffeur awkwardly opened his door to exit the vehicle, exposing his chest. The man's right hand swiveled around, holding a large pistol. It stopped in midair when the first bullet shattered his heart. The second ripped a huge hole in the right lung. John neutralized the threat for self-preservation. He opened the back passenger door to search inside for any other occupants and found only the two.

With the targets neutralized, John searched the crowd for potential threats. People were running from the homeless man wielding the large handgun. He fired three rounds into the air to create more fear and confusion. Then, he nonchalantly walked away toward the subway station.

John's patience, planning, and practice had received their reward. Castellano's blood added another payment installment to balance the scales of justice.

John paused for a minute at the bottom of the stairs to look back to the street level. No one was following him. He turned down the hallway and looked again as an extra precaution. *Good. No one's following me.*

He heard the train coming down the tracks and noticed the flickering light getting brighter. His heart was pounding. The train pulled into the station. He leaped inside and sat down facing the entryway. Then, he watched the doors close, and the train began to lumber forward.

John exited the train at the next station and removed the hat, fake teeth, smelly raincoat, and wig. A nearby green painted trash can welcomed the new black bag's arrival for transport to the Freshkills sanitary landfill on Staten Island. When no one was watching, he turned the "I Love New York" sweatshirt inside out. It changed to an inconspicuous gray outer garment.

Back at the Cadillac, the police cordoned off a perimeter around the crime scene and waited for the detectives to gather evidence. They found little except the metal casings ejected by the murder weapon.

The coroner's report later concluded Castellano died instantly when a hollow-point bullet entered his head above the left eye. It expanded on impact as designed and ripped a large exit wound out the back of the skull. The report didn't say Castellano's head looked like the pictures of John F. Kennedy's head the coroner had studied back in medical school. Other remarks in the report said that the bodyguard in the back seat died from trauma sustained by two gunshot wounds in an attempt to withdraw his revolver. The chauffeur expired in the street, also from trauma sustained by two gunshot wounds.

The police scoured the area looking for witnesses, but the crowd who had watched the shooting vanished into the neighborhood. Residents in New York City had grown apathetic or calloused by the constant lawlessness.

The police interviewed the drivers of the vehicles surrounding the Cadillac. They described the assassin as a homeless-looking man with scruffy hair who wore a dirty raincoat and hat. One witness said he had seen a man stagger up to the Cadillac, then stop. Out of nowhere, he had pulled a gun and began firing at the car. Then, the man disappeared into the subway station across from the park on Fourteenth Street between Park Avenue and Fourth Avenue.

The police searched the subway station and didn't find any clues. They had no idea which direction the shooter had traveled. He just vanished into the city's underbelly.

After entering the subway system, John used countermeasures to prevent the NYPD from reconstructing his trail. He knew they shared their evidence with the Mafia, so first he traveled north, then boarded the 7 Train traveling east to Flushing, Queens. At the Jackson Heights Station, he exited the line and doubled back, transferring onto multiple lines on the way to the Staten Island Ferry Terminal. There, the adrenaline rush subsided, bringing an unusually dry sensation to his mouth, and he got very hungry. He looked at the clock. He had twenty-five minutes before the next ferry to St. George. Within minutes he was devouring a roast beef sandwich and pulling on a Pabst Blue Ribbon tallboy.

When John arrived at the Browns, he found Margret reading a book in the living room. Betty was sleeping soundly on the couch like an angel. He retrieved another Pabst from the refrigerator. She sipped her Earl Grey tea and asked, "How was your evening in the city?"

John answered, "It was good. I finished what I came to do. I even stopped and spent some time drinking a cup of coffee while sitting on a park bench. Seems like the traffic gets worse every time I come back. Cars and trucks stacked together bumper to bumper. I ended up taking the subway all over town."

The next morning, Betty and Margret drove John to Newark Airport for the flight home to Kansas. Betty was sad watching John gather his luggage from the trunk. He noticed and gave her a big, loving hug goodbye and a kiss on the forehead. He knew it would cheer her spirit. Her smile confirmed it. Teary-eyed Margret hugged him and gave him a kiss on the cheek.

The mutual family bond had begun many years before, on the day the two sisters held John as a newborn baby. Over the following years, one of John's special memories with Margret and Betty was when they attended Jack's funeral at Arlington National

Colter's Code

Cemetery in Washington, DC. Their effort to make the journey touched John's heart and instilled an enduring feeling of gratitude for their kindness to honor his brother.

Betty had cried at the funeral, unable to grasp why her good friend Jack, someone she dearly loved, had died in some faraway jungle place called Vietnam. She watched intently as the six horses pulled the caisson carrying Jack's casket and wondered why the one horse led by the handsome soldier didn't have a rider. She especially liked the seven young men in the shiny uniforms standing near the casket with rifles raised. That was, until they scared her by firing a twenty-one-gun salute to their fallen hero. Loud noises always frightened her. John, like a big brother, held her hand until the tears stopped. Debbie, Jack, and Lori joined with hugs, forming a circle of love.

John arrived home in Kansas to a warm welcome that lifted his spirits. Taking another man's life was difficult and emotionally draining, but it had to be done. That night, he asked Debbie after the children fell asleep, "What would you think about visiting the Browns more often? It would be good for the kids. Margret and Betty are getting older and may not be with us much longer."

Debbie agreed that the whole family should experience more of Betty and Margret's loving spirit.

Chapter 18
The River

John's war against the Mafia wasn't over. Joey Provenzano had flaunted his freedom long enough from the evidence that demanded a righteous verdict.

It was time for the final act of retribution against the Genovese crime family. In John's mind, he didn't think of himself as a vigilante but as a servant of righteousness charged with using his talents and abilities against unabated evil. He was guided by his code to stand up against injustice. Now, he would resume his quest to balance the scales of justice and wield Justitia's sword to restore the equilibrium.

He understood protecting his identity was paramount during his crusade against the Mafia. It required careful planning with random patterns of deception and countermeasures. He believed he had waited long enough to establish a time gap that prevented any connection between Sal's punishment, the robberies, and justice for Castellano.

The idea for the next attack plan had been planted during that chance meeting last Christmas at the Chart House in Weehawken, New Jersey. The restaurant was one of Joey's go-to meeting places to conduct business. There, John would deliver his own final installment.

After Castellano joined his Mafia family in hell, Angelo Galante was promoted to boss of the Genovese crime family. He was connecting the dots and knew somehow the hit on Sal, the robberies, and now the hit on Castellano were connected. He didn't know how yet, but he knew he'd find the answer. To sweeten the incentives, he increased the reward for any information leading to the identity of Castellano's assassin. His psychopathic mind thought, *When I get this motherfucker, I'm gonna enjoy every scream. And every time he begs for mercy, I'll torture him some more. After he tells me where his family is, I'll kill them too. Just because I can.*

Since Angelo now controlled the powerful Genovese empire in the New York metropolitan area, he enlisted every resource to find Castellano's killer. His frustration morphed into an obsession as time passed without a lead. His distress was like a forest fire consuming everything in its path. He kept thinking, *We need to find this guy. But how? He's like a fucking ghost. He just disappears without a trace. If I can just figure out the motive, I can find this guy. Then, he'll tell me everything I want to know, including who he's working for.*

Angelo mentally revisited the facts of the hits and robberies one more time, hoping to find a connection. He recalled that when Sal was hit, the lone gunman had used a highly sophisticated flash-bang grenade. The bank at the Blind Dog Bar was also robbed by a lone gunman who used a flash-bang grenade. Then, he reexamined the Castellano hit.

He summarized in his mind, *The shooter's a stone-cold killer who works alone. He's an expert marksman with special skills in explosives, disguises, and evasion techniques.* Angelo had an idea. *I know how to find someone like that. I'll contact Eddie Warren, Castellano's guy at the CIA. With his resources in the government, he'll find this guy.*

The meeting took place on a secluded bench in Central Park under two tall elm trees. A squirrel was scurrying around looking for some food and jumped up on the bench next to Warren. Warren took a bite of his sandwich and ripped off some roast beef to feed the fluffy-tailed creature. Angelo watched in disbelief as the squirrel nibbled the tasty morsel from his hand without biting him.

Warren began by saying, "I was sorry to hear about Castellano. He and I have worked together ever since World War II. He helped save a lot of American lives in Sicily and the rest of Europe. It was a small price to pay years later when I gave him Kennedy's itinerary in Dallas. That got a little messy with your man Ruby shooting Oswald. What a patsy Oswald was. No one ever proved your sniper on the grassy knoll made the kill shot.

"So, you're Angelo. Castellano told me about you. He said you're in the Black Hand and described your special skills at torture and killing with extreme prejudice. Would you ever consider doing a special job for the government from time to time?"

Angelo just stared and said, "Maybe. Right now, we want to know if anyone in the government was involved in the hits on Sal and Castellano."

Warren answered, "Castellano had asked me to make some inquires when Sal was hit, but I didn't find anything. Then after I found out Castellano was assassinated by someone outside of the Mafia, I started a new search within the government. I knew only the most powerful people in the United States government could have commanded the resources necessary to kill the godfather of the New York Mafia. My contacts found nothing. No government agency was officially or unofficially involved.

"Then I wondered if someone was operating secretly within the government who had a vendetta against the Genovese crime organization. Like maybe a Kennedy loyalist who found out your guy took him out in Dallas. When I didn't find a thing, I decided to reach out to the people on the dark side of the government. You know, off-the-books kind of stuff where we employ the really scary people. That's when I found some golden nuggets for you.

"My contacts gave me files on a handful of people they employ. Trained killers with the extraordinary level of intelligence, training, and other skill sets necessary to conduct those kinds of operations and disappear without a trace. The government also employs outside independent specialists—contractors, basically. There're assassins from the dark side who commit indescribable atrocities sanctioned by the highest levels of government. Here, I made a list for you. I hope it helps."

Angelo smiled when he read the combined list of the elite warriors. He was confident it contained his ghost.

***

Back in Kansas, John was returning to his routine, which started with an early-morning six-mile run followed by breakfast with the family, then work at the university. As he jogged, John thought about his plan for Joey. He knew the next opportunity would be during the school's summer break, when the Colters always visited Linda. It was part of an informal commitment to support her with love and provide a distraction from her loneliness. The loss of her husband and now only child had brought a dispirited existence to her once-vibrant household. Linda's career helped as a diversion, and volunteering at a local food bank brought her a feeling of goodness, especially when encountering those less fortunate. But the visits from the Colters lifted her spirits and gave her hope like nothing else could.

As part of the healing process, Linda had thought about selling the house to avoid the constant memory of that painful day, but in the end, she knew other happy memories there helped sustain her one day at a time. If she moved, she feared that over time, those reminders would disappear and be erased by the activities of a new life. She endured the pain to remember the joy of each day she had shared with her husband and daughter.

The day came and the Colters arrived at Linda's house. John initiated the next phase of his war against the Mafia. He called an old friend from high school, Bruce Allen, and invited him to meet for drinks. He needed a reason to return to the Chart House in Weehawken and he knew Bruce liked a cocktail after a stressful day at work to relax. As an added enticement, the restaurant was conveniently located on Bruce's commute home from the investment bank Brown Brothers Harriman in Manhattan.

John arrived first and selected two seats at the far end of the bar. He wanted an area with dim lighting that obscured his visibility from the other patrons. He didn't need to be recognized by Joey while performing reconnaissance at the bar. The Crown Royal with a splash of Diet Coke arrived, and John sipped the refreshing libation while waiting for Bruce. He arrived ten minutes later and ordered a martini with three blue-cheese olives. After cheerful greetings, the conversation turned to the new events since their last meeting. As always, the conversation changed as they reminisced about the good old days.

Two drinks later, John noticed Joey with a group of tough-looking guys entering the front door. Bingo. As John had hoped, Joey regularly visited the bar. The bartender confirmed it was Joey's favorite hangout by shouting their names and welcoming them like conquering heroes.

Bruce asked, "So John, what's with the beard and glasses? Do I see a little gray in there? You look older. Is Father Time catching up to you?"

John replied, "Gray! Is it that noticeable?"

Bruce said, "Oh. And I like the causal college professor look. Nice polo shirt and blue jeans. Changing subjects, how's your company doing? I still get the million-dollar deposit every quarter to your investment account at the firm."

John said, "I hope you invest it wisely for me." Then he added humbly, "You know what, Bruce? It's a great joy to read the letters from so many people who now swim in the ocean with their families and friends without the fear of sharks. That means more to me than the money." He paused. He didn't like braggards but added, "The company's doing great with record sales and profits. If you can believe this, we just landed an account in Australia. Next year, I'm planning an extreme hiking expedition deep in the Outback."

Colter's Code

Bruce responded, "That's awesome. I hope you write one of those adventure series articles and send me a copy. I love reading about your crazy encounters. That grizzly bear story was the best."

John slapped Bruce on the shoulder and replied, "You should come with me to Australia. Tell the firm you're entertaining a client."

John looked over at Joey. *I wonder. Did my change in appearance work? Does he recognize me?* He sipped his Crown Royal. Then, he noticed Joey was staring right at him. Tense seconds passed. John turned to ask Bruce about his investment account and nervously looked back. *Good*, he thought. *Joey didn't recognize me.*

Off and on, John glanced at Joey hoping to gain valuable intelligence about his habits. *That's interesting. He disappears around the corner with some business associates and later returns to the bar. That's where I saw him on the couch the last time I was here.* He excused himself to go to the men's restroom, and around the corner, there was Joey sitting on a couch talking to an associate. John made the return trip from the men's bathroom and Joey was still there.

He rejoined the conversation with Bruce, but within minutes a drunken patron started yelling and swearing at his girlfriend, who was sitting next to John. The argument escalated to the point where the drunk pushed her. She lost her balance and caromed off John, simultaneously spilling her drink in his lap. At first, John casually wiped off his wet jeans with some paper bar napkins and added a forgiving comment. But then, things changed from bad to worse. The boyfriend grew more belligerent, and she began to cry.

John had had enough and said, "Miss, do you need some help?"

The boyfriend shouted at John, "Mind your own goddamn business."

John stood up and answered, "It's my business now. I won't allow you to bully and disrespect a woman like that."

Then, the boyfriend grabbed her arm and squeezed it so tightly she screamed, "Stop it, you're hurting me!"

The soon-to-be ex-boyfriend yelled, "Shut up, you fucking bitch. You're coming with me."

John stepped forward to intervene and firmly said, "Let the lady go!"

Bruce was watching the boyfriend's aggressive body language and warned him by saying, "Don't do it, buddy. You'll just make him mad."

Bruce remembered John being bullied and humiliated as one of the fattest kids in school. He had witnessed John's transformation over the years into a tough, muscular defender of the other persecuted students. He knew John was going to defend this woman he didn't even know without fear or hesitation. No one bullied John anymore, and he wouldn't allow any man to hurt a woman.

The drunken boyfriend didn't listen and punched John below his left eye. John's head jolted backward. He shook his head and quickly recovered. That's when Bruce noticed that changed look in John eyes. John's return punch hit the boyfriend's jaw so hard it sent a lightning bolt of pain through his head like he'd been hit with a sledgehammer. John added a rapid right uppercut that landed the boyfriend on the floor. When his eyes opened, he saw spinning stars above his head and asked, "Where am I?"

Joey and two Mafia associates heard the commotion and returned to the bar in time to witness the fight. It didn't last long.

One of Joey's men said, "Hey man, you some kinda boxer? That combination of punches was impressive. I've seen a lot of guys hit really hard, but your power was something else."

John replied, "Thank you. No, I'm not. I just like to stay in shape. I run a lot and lift weights."

Pointing to the boyfriend on the floor, the man said, "He shouldn't hurt a woman like that."

Joey looked at John and asked, "You look familiar, you guys from around here?"

Mark E. Uhler

John answered, "No, sir, I'm visiting from the Midwest. My friend here works in the city as an investment banker. We're just here for a few drinks. I love the view across the river."

Joey added, "My name is Joey. That bum deserved it." He turned and commanded, "Anthony, get that drunk out of here. Tell him Joey said don't ever come in here again."

"You got it, boss," the soldier answered.

John responded, "I'm John," shaking Joey's hand. "This is my friend Bruce."

Joey said, "Nice to meet you guys. Hey Mikey, their drinks are on me. Give them whatever they want." On his way back to his seat, Joey said to one of his men, "Too bad that guy's from out of town. I could use another tough guy that hits like that."

John appreciated Joey's gesture to pay their bar tab. It wouldn't change the outcome of their next meeting.

On the way out, Bruce and John thanked Joey for the drinks and exited, saying their goodbyes in the parking lot.

As Bruce drove away, John remained to reconnoiter the outside of the restaurant. His main purpose was to find an escape route. He looked in every direction, thinking there were few choices. Chart House was located on a narrow strip of land jutting out from the main road. Three sides were surrounded by water, leaving only the driveway in and out. John thought to himself, *The driveway won't work. There's a clear line of sight from the front door to the main road. Anyone attempting to escape down that driveway is an easy target. That would be suicide. I need to find a safer way to escape.*

***

The Kansas Colters returned home from the vacation at Linda's, and John continued to formulate his attack plan for Joey.

Months passed before John decided it was time. To start the wheels in motion, he bought a nondescript van from a used car dealer on South Rangeline Road in Joplin, Missouri. He paid with untraceable Ben Franklins.

The seller said, "I'll need your name for my sales records and to write it on the title to record the transfer of ownership."

John cocked his head and asked, "Is that really necessary?" He pulled out a roll of Bens from his pants pocket. He stopped at six, when the seller decided a name was not necessary.

The cover story this time was another hiking adventure in the remote desert of Canyonlands National Park. It was located one hundred miles south of Moab, Utah, and seventy miles west. If anyone asked detailed questions about the desert excursion, he could answer by recalling events from a trip he had made there three years earlier.

John loaded his Jeep with enough camping equipment, food, and water to survive a week living in the desert. The usual stuff, such as his trusty six-inch Buck knife, the large Osprey backpack, lightweight two-person tent, sleeping bag, compass, first aid kit, inflatable sleeping mat, triangle cooking stove with propane canisters for fuel, water purification system, and the various other equipment necessary to sustain life in the harsh desert environment.

On Monday, he drove the Jeep to an old friend's remote barn near Pierce City, Missouri. There, he transferred all the gear to the van and resumed the drive down the interstate highway system east toward Virginia. Late that night, he stopped at a rest stop in Ohio to catch some shut-eye. Dreamland didn't last long. John woke when a tractor trailer rumbled past to resume its trek east to deliver its load.

In West Virginia, the radio music faded into static, and John turned the black tuning dial until he found an oldies station. He always felt nostalgic listening to the songs of his youth. He perked up and was singing along when the station played the song "Laughing." It was recorded by the band The Guess Who. The song reminded him of meeting his first love on a dream date back in high school.

The radio music ended at the train station in Tyson's Corner, Virginia. The mid-morning train left on schedule destined for Union Station in Washington, DC. There, the layover afforded John an opportunity to enjoy fish and chips with a refreshing pint of Guinness at the nearby Dubliner Irish Pub.

The northbound train from Union Station to New York City arrived at the platform at 3:13 p.m. Within minutes, John fell asleep wedged against the seat and window. In New York, he walked to a southbound subway station, boarded the subway car, and was whisked away to the Staten Island Ferry Terminal, and then to the Browns.

The front door opened, and John said, "Margret, it's good to see you again."

She answered, "It's good to see you, John. Come in." She smiled and gave him a warm hug as she announced, "Betty. Look who's here."

Inside, he turned and said, "Hi, Betty. How are you?"

Meekly, she replied, "Hello, John." He gave her the usual bear hug. Her excited smile lit up the room like a morning sunrise on a cloudless day.

John's duffel bag was packed to the gills with an assortment of casual clothing for a fall trip to New York City and a new disguise to wear to his rendezvous with Joey. Buried inside was a Barretta nine-millimeter pistol, three loaded clips, a box of fifty rounds of ammunition, a scuba diving mask, and other traveling essentials.

Tuesday afternoon, John took the train and ferry back to Manhattan for a final fact-finding mission. At the first stop, he devoured one of the towering pastrami sandwiches at Katz's Delicatessen. His belly bulged as he traveled across the Hudson River from the Thirty-Ninth Street New York Waterway ferry terminal to the Lincoln Harbor ferry terminal on the New Jersey side of the Hudson. Once there, he visually inspected the docking area, parking lots, ingress and egress from the street, adjacent piers, buildings, and places to hide. He recorded the mental images he needed and took the short walk to Chart House. There, he reexamined the perimeter and the waterway along the river's edge. His mind was putting the pieces of the puzzle together as he formulated the action plan and order of events. He confidently whispered to himself, *This is where I'll do it, and there's where I'll make my escape.*

John hailed a cab on the return trip to the Browns for a detour to pick up takeout at Joe's Italian Restaurant. He ordered a large Caesar salad and family-style lasagna with meatballs. The Brown sisters smiled from ear to ear as he entered the door. They had recognized the name on the bag and smelled the savory aroma. John knew they loved eating Joe's lasagna. It was the best in the city, but, at their age and in their physical condition, it was just too difficult for them to make the trip.

They enjoyed a treat for dessert. The layers of yellow shortcake were divided by white whipped cream. The top was covered in luscious white frosting dotted with bright-red strawberries.

On Wednesday evening, John's plan came to fruition. On the walk from the Liberty Harbor ferry, he joined a couple he met on the way who had dinner reservations at Chart House. They were excited to celebrate their first wedding anniversary and unknowingly helped John appear like one of the other eager diners.

John wore a gray business suit and a white button-down collared shirt accentuated by a blue Brooks Brothers tie. The shiny black dress shoes completed the attire for the evening. He entered the bar, discovered more newfound friends, and ordered a Pabst Blue Ribbon beer.

From there, he watched Joey's Mafia crew at the opposite end pounding down drink after drink, laughing and carousing. Within minutes, Joey appeared from around the corner to join his band of boisterous criminals.

Joey disappeared around the corner again, and John followed him to take a trip to the bathroom. He needed relief from the beers.

John exited the restroom and rounded the corner. Joey was still sitting there on the couch talking to two of his men. They didn't pay attention to the businessman casually walking toward them until he suddenly reached underneath his jacket and a deadly handgun appeared at eye level.

Just then, two more of Joey's crew members walked around the other corner from the bar. They were startled at first to witness a guy pointing a large handgun at their boss. The alert one reached for his own weapon but his hesitation from fear slowed his reaction long enough for John to fire one round into his right shoulder. The bullet's impact spun him around like a top as the hollow point expanded and tore through the muscles. His weapon flew into the air and fell harmlessly onto the floor.

John's eyes searched for the next threatening target and instinctively aimed at the other man standing near the bar's entrance. The man flinched as John's gun barrel turned toward him and he defensively leaped behind a wall for safety. John pivoted left to aim his weapon to kill Joey, who was still sitting on the couch, but the opportunity had vanished. One of Joey's companions shielded his boss from the assassin as the other reached for the Smith & Wesson in his shoulder holster.

Realizing he was in mortal danger, John dashed toward the front door as he fired three shots into the ceiling to create more panic and confusion. It worked. The loud gunshot blasts in the confined hallway momentarily stopped Joey's men from responding. John rounded the corner, and as he did, he knocked down a woman standing by the hostess. The other patrons parted like the Red Sea, and he sped out the front door.

Joey's remaining crew in the bar area withdrew their pistols and looked for the source of the gunshots. Not finding one, they cautiously turned the corner into the entryway. The frightened hostess yelled, "A big guy just ran out the door that way with a gun!" Two soldiers chased the fugitive out the door.

Two other armed soldiers from Joey's crew met them outside. One chirped, "Where the hell did this guy go?"

They paired off. Two men went north with their revolvers aiming into the parking lot, hunting for the target. The other pair swept south and then circled behind the restaurant. The northern pair found nothing and stopped, waiting, listening, and watching for any movement.

One man in the back spotted John and yelled, "There he is. We got him." He pointed at the guy running toward the Hudson. Then he said, "We can trap him at the edge of the river and kill him."

John's original escape plan had involved exiting out the back door. There, he would strip off the business suit and throw it in the dumpster. Underneath his suit, he was wearing a thin black neoprene scuba diving suit. The plan was to slip away undetected in the murky waters of the Hudson River.

Change of plans. No time for that now. I got to haul it to the river, he said to himself. John paused at the water's edge to take off his suit jacket and slip on a scuba mask.

As he stopped, they opened fire. John heard the sound of bullets zipping by his head.

He took a deep breath and dove straight down under the surface of the water.

At the river's edge, the chasing gunmen had noticed the target put something on his head and then vanished. When they reached the riverbank, he was gone. *Where did the guy go?* they thought to themselves. They looked north and south along the bulkhead. No one.

"Look, he's there in the water," one shouted. He pointed to bubbles rising to the surface, lit faintly in the night by the city lights. They fired their pistols again and again. Underwater, John swam as fast as he could manage, then suddenly he felt intense pain in his shoulder. Alarmed, he paused to ascertain the source of the pain. A second jolt of pain emanated from the back of his right leg.

He thought, *I can't believe I'm hit.* He endured the pain, pushing through and swimming southward to his extraction point.

The gunmen stood at the river's edge. They waited and watched, expecting a body to surface. It didn't, and when the bubbles disappeared, they gave up their search and went inside to tell Joey they had shot the guy and he drowned.

Joey asked, "Did you see any blood or a body?"

"No. The river's current must have swept the body into the bay, or maybe it sank."

Joey was furious. "What do you mean, 'no'? How the hell do you even know you hit the guy? You two dumbasses get out of my sight." Then he thought, *I know I've seen that guy before. But where?*

The river's current carried John to an isolated pier just north of the ferry terminal. There, he grabbed a ladder and looked around. He painfully hauled himself up out of the water.

He stripped off his soaked business suit and water-filled shoes. He wondered how badly he was wounded and reached to touch the back shoulder of his wetsuit. *That's good, no blood*, he said to himself. Next, he twisted and inspected his leg. There was no blood, only the throbbing pain. *The water must have slowed the bullets*, he thought. Then, John found the bag of clothes he had conveniently hidden the previous night.

Mark E. Uhler

The ferryboat parted the choppy waters crossing the Hudson River to Manhattan's West Side. He was disappointed the plan failed but relieved he had not sustained serious injuries.

Two days later, John limped onto a southbound train in Grand Central Terminal and started his journey home. The dark black bruises surrounded by red circles reminded him his life had almost ended in a dark, watery grave. Safety waited for John in Kansas.

Chapter 19
Skiing in Vermont

Debbie paused in the bathroom doorway John's first night back. She was wearing sexy pink see-through Victoria's Secret lingerie for a special welcome-home present. John was lustfully aroused. She approached him with a seductive saunter but stopped with apprehension when he removed his shirt. A gigantic yellowish-black bruise spread across the back of his shoulder.

Alarmed, she shouted, "What happened to your shoulder?"

John proceeded to summarize what happened. He had aborted his plan when two of Joey's crew unexpectedly rounded the corner. He knew he was outnumbered and that the odds of failure were overwhelming, so he had escaped out the front door and circled behind the building thinking he could make it to the water's edge before they discovered him. He was wrong.

After he dove into the river, he resurfaced to inhale another breath of fresh air. Two gunmen suddenly showed up on the dock intending to kill him. He plunged back under the water to avoid their hail of bullets, but one hit his shoulder and another his leg.

Debbie was relieved the wounds weren't worse. She loved John and supported his quest to balance the scales of justice but didn't want him to pay the ultimate price like his brother Jack.

Debbie's concern made John wonder, *Are the risks to my family too great? Sal Provenzano and Philip Castellano received their righteous judgment. Isn't that enough?*

No, he resolved. *Joey remains a free man. He must be held accountable for his actions.*

The aborted attempt compelled John to formulate a new plan. He called his old buddy Andy for help. Andy's phone rang and he answered, "This is Officer Morgan with the Maplewood Police Department. How can I help you?"

"Andy, this is John," he said. "Hey, when you first called me about Amy's shooting, you offered to help me. Well, I need some information about Joey Provenzano."

Lowering his voice and glancing around the station to see if anyone was listening, Andy answered, "Of course, I'll help. What would you like to know?"

John replied, "What can you tell me about his lifestyle? Where he lives? Is he under any formal investigation for his criminal activities? Stuff like that."

Andy said, "He's not the subject of any investigation that I know of. But I'll check around. We knew a lot about his dad, Sal, because he loved media attention. But Joey, he's the opposite. He lives a pretty quiet life. I do know two of Joey's crew members were found shot to death in Stony Brook Park. You know the one, it's near Watchung Lake, just off Mountain Boulevard in Watchung. Word on the street was Joey's crew threatened to burn down a German restaurant located on Route 22 over in North Plainfield if they didn't make some extortion payments. Turns out the owner of the restaurant was in the German American Bund, which is basically the remnants of the Nazi Party. When World War II broke out, law enforcement officials in New Jersey thought they'd eradicated the Nazi Party. But after the war, many high-ranking powerful Nazi officials secretly immigrated into northern New Jersey and went underground. The New Jersey elements of the Ku Klux Klan were instrumental in helping them, and they developed a special bond.

"I read a couple of police bulletins reporting some of those Nazis were former SS assassins who'd hunted and butchered Jews in France and Belgium during the war. The SS were the most feared and ruthless killers on Earth. Now they protect Bund members. They're so violent, the Mafia in New York and New Jersey avoid antagonizing or threatening any member of the Bund. I guess Joey's crew didn't do their homework and threatened the wrong people. We're not sure whether the Klan killed the guys from Joey's crew or whether it was SS assassins. We do know the men were tortured for days before they were brutally hacked to death.

"There is one interesting piece of information about Joey. We discovered he owns a log cabin in the woods on Stratton Mountain in Vermont. The FBI reported the five New York families held a retreat on the property a couple of months ago. The log cabin is located about a quarter mile down a one-lane gravel road through the woods. Agents tried approaching with cameras to take photographs but had to retreat. Luckily, they spotted the perimeter guards before they got shot for trespassing. It's like the Wild West up in those moun—"

John interrupted, "Do you know how often Joey goes up there?"

Andy responded, "The information we have is he goes up there almost every weekend in the winter to ski at the Stratton Mountain Ski Resort. It's right near his cabin. Joey still lives here in New Jersey, at 349 Prosper Terrace in East Orange."

The conversation migrated to questions about each other's families and careers and ended with friendly goodbyes. Andy stared at the telephone after he set the receiver down. His policeman's trained mind kicked into gear, and he began to question John's motives. *Even though John's my friend, I wonder why he's so interested in Joey. What is John up to? Whatever it is, I'll help him do it. No one will ever know we had this conversation.*

John was grateful to Andy for telling him about Joey's log cabin in Vermont and that he loved to ski Stratton Mountain on weekends in the winter. He thought to himself, *That's a really remote area of New England. Maybe I can settle the score with Joey in Vermont.*

The Colters' next trip to New York City was for Christmas. John had grown a thick beard and now looked like a mountain man fresh off the movie set of *Jeremiah Johnson*. The family loved it, especially Debbie in the privacy of their bedroom.

He decided to change tactics because up close and personal was too dangerous. He purchased a deer-hunting rifle and drove twice a week to a shooting range. There he religiously practiced firing the new Remington 30-06 rifle. He knew it was the same caliber as the M1 rifle given to many American soldiers to kill Germans and Japanese during World War II. He thought, *It did the job then, and I'll use it to do the job now.* He attached a Leopold scope he had bought at a gun show in Wichita, Kansas. The scope paid dividends and dramatically improved John's accuracy. He hit the bullseye nine out of ten times from a distance of one hundred yards. He was ready.

The holiday season arrived, and John planned a family outing in Manhattan as part of their Christmas traditions. A cold front arrived from Canada, bringing with it a wintery mix of freezing rain and snow. Rather than fight the snarled-up traffic, the Colters rode an Erie Lackawanna train to Penn Station. It was conveniently located under Madison Square Garden at Seventh Avenue and Thirty-Fourth Street, a stone's throw away from their first stop, which was Macy's. Inside, they gazed at the spectacular lobby decorations, which filled their hearts with Christmas cheer. Outside, they marveled at the mechanical window displays and recorded Christmas music that resonated through the air.

A yellow cab swept the merry band to Grand Central Terminal on Park Avenue and Forty-Second Street. There, the family was filled with wonder as they witnessed the majestic architecture of the old train station and walked through the maze of magnificent corridors and platforms. Young Jack and Lori especially adored the brass clock with four opal faces centered below the zodiac ceiling of the main concourse.

They finished lunch inside the terminal and whisked their way outside to hail another cab to avoid the winter elements on their way to the next adventure at the Federal Reserve Bank of New York. John had a friend who had arranged a private tour of the gold vault. It stored more gold than Fort Knox.

Inside the Federal Reserve building, the elevator descended several stories into the granite warehouse below the main lobby. The doors opened, exposing a ninety-ton steel cylinder door protecting the only entry point into the vault. The half-a-million gold bars silently greeted them.

The vault's custodian invited the Colters inside, where he picked up a gold bar from an enormous stack. He handed the bar to Jack and another to Lori and said, "Each bar weighs twenty-seven pounds. Don't drop it. That's why I wear special steel-toed shoes. Here, look—you can see a dent in this one." For an extra treat, he unlocked a side door, exposing a large rectangular room. They were awestruck. It was filled with gold bars stacked from the floor to the tall ceiling.

Debbie curiously asked, "How much gold is in all these vaults?"

He answered, "Over $28 billion at today's price of gold."

After the Christmas holiday season ended, Debbie, Jack, and Lori returned home to Kansas. John flew east to Boston. It was part of his plan, his alibi. He told everyone he had always wanted to fulfill his dream of standing on all four corners of the forty-eight contiguous United States. As part of the ruse, he planned to hike the northernmost part of the Appalachian Trail.

John's adventures over many years had brought him to three of the four corners. In college, he had visited friends in Washington and hiked to Cape Flattery. A few years later, John had peered through the fence into Mexico while standing in Border Field State Park, just south of Coronado Beach, California. It was the southwest tip of the United States. Standing at the southeast tip had occurred on a scuba diving expedition to Key West, Florida. He had celebrated by consuming a few too many drinks at Sloppy Joe's, but he had to go there. It had been Hemingway's favorite watering hole.

The fourth and final corner was located near the Upper Saint John River Valley near Hamlin, Maine. John rented a car at Logan Airport in Boston and drove seven hours north. When he arrived, he looked east across the border into Canada, then smiled as he felt a sense of humility and accomplishment. He recognized that few Americans would ever experience standing on all four corners of the United States.

With the trek to the fourth corner completed, John parked the rental at the Appalachian Trailhead at Mount Katahdin, Maine. He hiked a portion of the trail and then rendezvoused with a truck driver to procure transportation to Vermont. The driver worked for Steve Winters, an old friend of John's who owned a trucking company that delivered Cabot Cheese products all over the Northeast. John had previously asked Winters if he could hitch a ride to hike some of the mountains scattered across New England. Winters was happy to help. John knew that way, it would be impossible to trace him to the crime scene.

The driver delivered his passenger just off Vermont Highway 7 in Manchester as instructed. From there, John walked into town to purchase additional camping supplies at Mountain Goat Outfitters. He needed a small propane canister for cooking, some prepackaged dried meals, and a map of the Stratton Mountain trails. While inside, he noticed a pair of webbed wooden snowshoes hanging on the wall. He thought to himself, *These might come in handy if I have to make a fast getaway traipsing through the snow-covered mountain.* They made the trip.

Now that John was fully supplied, he began to hike up the road toward the trailhead on Town Highway 26.

Chapter 20
The Mountain

John cherished ascending the side of the mountain through the piney woods and listening to the wind whistling through the treetops. At the Stratton Pond campsite, he shoveled two-foot-deep snow to make a clearing on the frozen forest floor and pitch his base camp tent. Inside, John unpacked the special equipment needed to complete his mission. First, he assembled the Remington rifle, attached the high-powered Leopold scope, and added a silencer. For ammunition, he had procured special cartridges manufactured with smokeless and flash-less gunpower to help conceal the source of the rifle's report.

Nightfall escorted colder temperatures into the forest, falling to minus five degrees Fahrenheit. John had planned ahead, and he survived the cold by hunkering down inside his sleeping bag manufactured to protect its inhabitants to minus twenty. Morning breakfast was cooked over the small triangle propane stove. He savored every bite of the scrambled eggs with cheese and sausage. His nostrils enjoyed the tantalizing aroma of steaming hot coffee.

It was time. He boiled snow for extra drinking water to remain hydrated and loaded his backpack with the essential gear to transverse Stratton Mountain to the ski slopes.

Colter's Code

The hike across the deep snow was exhausting but rewarding. He found the perfect location to stalk his prey and to peruse the field of fire.

After John reconnoitered the slopes with his binoculars, he buried his backpack in the snow and emerged to find the ski lift access point. He was wearing a blue ski jacket with matching pants, gloves, and Carrera goggles. At the lift, he hopped on a chair for the descent to the resort's little village. He needed to locate an observation point to wait and find Joey.

At the bottom, he joined a young couple sitting on a bench near the entryway.

John asked, "Do you mind if I join you?"

The girl answered, "Not at all, have a seat. Where're you from?"

John replied, "I'm from the Midwest, near Kansas City. It's my first time skiing. Where are you folks from?"

Peter said, "Wow, you're a long way from home. We drove up yesterday from Boston."

John responded, "Boston. That Game Seven loss to the Reds sure was a tough one. It was one of the greatest World Series ever played. Are you guys Red Sox fans?"

She answered, "Peter is. His dad is a season-ticket holder, so we go to a lot of games. Peter's a student at BC—Boston College, that is—and I'm studying nursing at Boston University."

Mark E. Uhler

John said, "Really? My wife Debbie graduated from nursing school."

Peter asked, "What do you do out there in the Midwest?"

John answered, "Currently, I teach economics classes at Pittsburg State University, but I grew up in New Jersey and spent a lot of summers vacationing in Harwich Port on Cape Cod."

Peter said, "My parents own a house in Harwich Port at the end of Zylpha Road right on the beach. Where did you stay?"

John replied, "We rented a cabin at the Seadar Inn by the Sea near Wychmere Harbor. I walked by your parents' house a few times on my way to Allen Harbor. Years ago, Mrs. Ashton—she's the kind lady who owns the house at the harbor's entrance—used to give me permission to perform swan dives off their private dock."

Peter asked, "That mansion with the ocean view and huge yacht?"

John answered, "Yes. That's the one."

The couple excused themselves to ski down the black runs and John waited patiently, hoping to find Joey. He needed to know what color outfit he was wearing on the slopes to make a positive identification. Shooting an innocent skier by mistake was not an option.

John thought since it was noontime, Joey would take a break to eat lunch before more skiing that afternoon. To pass the time, he watched the beginners attending ski school, learning braking and other skills. He marveled at how fearlessly the youngsters glided across the snow.

Joey appeared thirty minutes later wearing black ski boots, an orange ski jacket, blue pants, Oakley sunglasses, and a blue sock hat. He grabbed his skis from the nearby rack and boarded a lift chair to ascend the mountain and resume skiing.

Now that John had acquired his target, he returned to the hidden backpack and slipped on white camouflage coveralls, a mask, a hat, and special hunting gloves. Slowly, he inched closer to the edge of the tree line. His snowlike appearance helped him move with stealth. He found a fallen pine tree that provided a position to stalk his target through his binoculars. From this distance he thought, *It's an easy shot to the ski lift drop-off point over there at the top.* He intently searched for Joey by watching the skiers ascend the mountain on ski lift chairs and hop off the seats to start their next runs, gracefully gliding down the slopes. *There. That's him. He's the guy wearing the orange jacket, blue pants, and blue hat sitting on a ski lift chair. The one next to those two skiers.*

John focused as they approached the top. He mounted the Remington on a log perch, pointing the barrel toward the ski lift chairs. He pulled the breechloader's bolt back, allowing the magazine's spring to load a cartridge, and then pushed the bolt forward to lock the chamber. He flipped the safety to the off position and slowly positioned his finger on the trigger. Next, he slowed his breathing to steady the gun barrel's figure-eight patten and align the crosshairs in the center of Joey's chest. He thought, *He's moving too fast in that chair. I might miss.* His lips whispered, *Wait, wait. He'll pause after he jumps off. That's when I'll take the shot.*

Then, he hesitated as he thought, *I'm not sure it's him. I can't tell.*

He didn't want to shoot the wrong man. John looked intently through the high-powered Leopold scope directly at the man's face. *I'm still not sure. Are those goggles Oakleys?*

He had no choice but to wait. The suspended chairs kept methodically arriving at the top and then turning to repeat the cycle of creeping down the mountain to retrieve the next batch of skiers. Soon enough, Joey jumped off the chair and his skies hit the snow. He extended both arms, stabbing his ski poles into the snow to gain balance and propel himself forward. Then, he stopped and looked around just as John had anticipated. Every skier paused there to gaze across the majestic snow-covered mountaintops. A minute later, he vanished.

John reconsidered his options. He thought about changing methods to kill Joey up close and personal using his long-bladed Buck knife. He could use the cover of darkness to find Joey.

John also considered killing Joey at his remote log cabin deep in the woods. It was winter, and it was cold. John surmised that every night, Joey would walk out the back door to gather firewood for the living room fireplace to heat the cabin. John could hide in the underbrush of the surrounding woods. That would provide an excellent rifle-firing position. As an added benefit, the Stratton Mountain map illustrated multiple nearby snowmobile trails available for avenues of escape. But that was the last choice. John didn't like the idea of Joey's family finding his gruesome dead body. They were innocent players in this war against the Mafia. Linda had found Amy downstairs: John didn't want Joey's wife to find her husband's bloody, dead body and have those mental images scarring her for life.

He wondered what the best option was. *I'm here now. I'll wait for Joey to return for another run down the slopes.* The reward came when Joey arrived on another ski lift chair, and John positively identified him. *All this time and all this planning. This is it*, he thought to himself.

John fired the first bullet into Joey's upper body. He watched through the Leopold scope as a spray of blood flew into the air behind the target's chest. Joey collapsed to the ground. John quickly chambered another round and positioned the crosshairs on the fallen target. He pulled the trigger, sending the second missile 4,080 feet per second into the body. Joey joined his father as the white snow turned red around the corpse.

***

Witnesses told the sheriff's deputies they hadn't heard a sound or noticed a flash. They had no clue what direction the shots had come from. The sheriff determined from the position of the body and blood splatter that the shots had originated from the tree line above the victim. He dispatched two deputies to investigate, and they found an indentation in the snow. It revealed the shooter's firing position. They searched the immediate area and found a deep indentation the size of a human arm. The deputies surmised that the clever marksman retrieved the spent bullet casings.

The deputies knew they had no time to linger and started following the fugitive's footprints in the snow. The ill-prepared deputies plodded toward the mountaintop. They hadn't brought snowshoes, and with each step, their knees sank below the surface of the snow. The hunt intensified as the sun disappeared behind the mountain peak and darkness slowly swallowed the light in its shadow. The chase slowed to a snail's pace as the physical demands of hiking through the deep snow sapped their strength. Physical fitness was not part of the Windham Sherriff Department's job description for a deputy.

Time was running out. Darkness was creeping through the forest to engulf them. They followed the footprints using flashlights until the falling and drifting snowflakes pushed by the howling wind nibbled away the tracks.

***

John hiked south along the ridgeline in the opposite direction of his base camp tent. The flashlights followed but diminished as the winter weather worsened. He stopped, read his compass, and identified the direction he was traveling. Then he turned west as a countermeasure. The snowshoes were a godsend, navigating across the deep layer of snow. He found a trail and rechecked the map to pinpoint his location. It was the trail that circled back to his tent.

After dinner, John battled the sub-zero winds to locate the middle of Stratton Pond. There, he chopped a hole through the thick blue ice. Kerplunk: the deep, dark water swallowed the rifle. Kerplunk: other evidence such as the scope, ammunition, and white camouflage clothing sank to the bottom where the mud swallowed them. John began shivering and returned to the campfire to raise his body temperature. Staring at the flames dancing above the burning logs, he suddenly experienced a tremendous feeling of accomplishment. His crusade for justice ended back on that ski slope. His war against the Mafia had ended in victory. *The good guys didn't finish last this time*, he said to himself.

Sal had lived by a code of evil that inflicted pain, suffering, and grief on his victims. His life ended abruptly on a city sidewalk. Castellano's reign of unpunished anarchy, corruption, and fear had been terminated in the back seat of his Fleetwood. Now, the final battle had ended with Joey's invitation to join the Mafia's special wing in hell.

John questioned himself, *Am I a hero or a villain? If I stood trial for my actions, would society judge me as a servant of righteousness or another lawless citizen seeking revenge motivated not by an honorable code but by hatred?*

The recognition of the answer concluded with a smile. He envisioned Lady Justice holding her scales. They had returned to equilibrium, and her sword was no longer held in an outstretched hand to deliver punishment. It was safely resting in its sheath.

John inspected Stratton Pond the next morning to confirm the hole in the ice was devoured by Mother Nature. The freezing temperatures had resealed the opening and the night's snowfall entombed its location.

The sheriff's hunt for the fugitive resumed at first light. Reinforcements had arrived from the state police and neighboring sheriffs' departments. The Windham County sheriff also procured four snowmobiles from the ski patrol to expedite the search. The sheriff had correctly guessed that the night's harsh weather would prevent the fugitive's escape. He said to the search teams, "The fugitive is on this mountain somewhere, and we're going to find him. Remember he is armed and extremely dangerous. He's already killed a skier with a high-powered rifle. Don't be his next victim.

"These snowmobiles go over sixty miles per hour, so be careful up there on the trails. I've assigned each pair of you a certain section of an organized grid on the map to search. We can cover the whole mountain in just a few hours. Now. Let's get this guy."

The search teams raced up the mountain to find the fugitive.

Just after sunrise, John packed his remaining gear and hiked to the Forest Service tower at the summit of Stratton Mountain. There, he climbed the stairs to the glass-encased observation room to enjoy the breathtaking, three hundred sixty-degree view of the Green Mountains. As an added joy, he watched the treetops dance to the rhythm of the wind as if the hand of God was brushing the hair of the forest.

The growing growl of an approaching machine interrupted the swooshing sound of wind whistling through the treetops. John digested the spectacular scenery for a few more minutes and started descending the fifty-six-foot-tall stairs. His hands almost froze grasping the cold steel railing.

On the way down, he noticed two uniformed sheriff's deputies. One was patiently sitting on his snowmobile holding a Glock nine-millimeter pistol while the other was searching through John's open backpack.

The disappointed deputies discovered only the equipment necessary to survive Vermont's brutal winter environment. The taller one said, "Hi. My name is Patrick Sanders. I'm a deputy with the Windham County Sheriff's Department. We're searching the mountain for a dangerous man who murdered a skier yesterday. Have you seen anybody up here the last few days?"

John answered, "No, deputy. I haven't noticed anybody. It's pretty cold and isolated in these mountains. That's why I hiked up here. I like to experience the serenity of the wilderness. I find it extremely comforting and spiritual and have gained a deep appreciation for the way Native Americans respected the earth and their special connection to nature."

The short round one asked, "Where're you from?"

John replied, "I'm from Pittsburg, Kansas." They looked confused. "It's south of Kansas City, Missouri," he added.

Colter's Code

The tall one responded, "You're a long way from Kansas, buddy. Can I see some kind of identification?"

"Absolutely," John said as he unzipped a pocket inside his jacket. He handed the deputy his driver's license.

"John Colter." The deputy said. He wrote the name and address down. "What do you do in Kansas for a living?"

John answered, "I'm a professor at Pittsburg State University. I teach economics."

The short one asked, "What are you doing in Vermont?"

John replied, "I'm hiking part of the Appalachian Trail up here in the Green Mountains. I usually hike out west along the Rocky Mountains or in the deserts in Utah and Arizona."

The tall one asked, "Where are you staying here in Vermont?"

John said, "You're pretty much looking at it. I'm camping along this part of the trail. I'm only up here for a few days to relax and enjoy the solitude and the beautiful scenery of the snow-covered mountains."

"What's your telephone number back in Kansas in case my boss, the sheriff, has some follow-up questions?" the tall one asked.

John answered, "It's 231-6716. Oh, the areas code's 316."

After a few more routine questions, the tall deputy handed John a card and said, "Be careful up here. If you see anyone suspicious or notice anything out of the ordinary, call the sheriff's number on this card."

John said, "I will. Any idea who this guy is?"

The deputy answered, "No, not yet. He got away in the blizzard last night. We've got teams searching all over this mountain and the surrounding area. He won't get far."

John responded, "Well, good luck. I hope you catch your fugitive."

Back in Manchester, John purchased the novel *The Winds of War* by Herman Wouk at the Northshire Bookstore to read on the return flight back to Kansas. The truck driver arrived at the original drop-off point and drove the mystery man back to Maine.

The same day, the sheriff began the process of investigating the leads developed during the search. He called the Pittsburg Police Department in Kansas.

A sergeant answered, "Hello, this is the Pittsburg Police Department, how may I help you?"

The sheriff replied, "This is Sheriff Calvin Newfane calling from Windham County, Vermont. I have a few questions about a man named John Colter who lives in Pittsburg. Is the police chief in?"

The sergeant placed him on hold and dialed the chief's extension. "Sir. You have a phone call on line two. The guy says he's a sheriff from up in Vermont somewhere and needs your help."

The chief answered, "This is Chief Billy Bob Porter. What can I help you with, sheriff?"

Newfane said, "Thank you for taking my call. I'm calling about a man from Pittsburg we interviewed during the hunt for a murder suspect on Stratton Mountain. As part of our investigation, I'm following up on our leads. What can you tell me about a man named John Colter?"

Porter replied, "You're joking, right? John Colter is a model citizen. Salt of the earth. I've known John a long time. Hell, he even trains with me at the police department's shooting range. He's an expert marksman with a nine-millimeter Barretta. We have friendly competitions from time to time, and he can outshoot me and all my officers. He owns a manufacturing plant here in Pittsburg. He started it back in college when he invented a small electrical device that prevents sharks from biting people swimming in the ocean. The plant employs over two hundred people with good-paying jobs. They're hard to come by in these parts. Two of his college buddies operate the business while he teaches economics classes at Pitt State. John donates a lot of his time and money to local charities, the chamber of commerce, United Way, Kiwanis Club, stuff like that. He serves as the chairman of the board of one charity. It's a foundation that helps over three hundred fifty residents with disabilities in the surrounding counties. What was he doing up in Vermont?"

Newfane answered, "He told one of my deputies that he was hiking part of the Appalachian Trail."

Porter responded, "That sounds like John. He goes hiking all over the country. The local paper even does a series of articles about his adventures. They're actually pretty captivating stories."

Newfane replied, "That's very helpful. Is there anything else you'd like to add?"

"Well, let me think," Porter said. After a pause, he added, "John is one of the smartest people I've ever met. He's also one of the kindest and nicest people I've had the pleasure of knowing. I can't believe he would have anything to do with a murder on Stratton Mountain."

Mrs. Montgomery announced late that afternoon, "Sheriff, you have a telephone call from Detective Miller in New Jersey. He said he needs to ask you some questions about suspects in the Joseph Provenzano shooting."

Back in New Jersey, Andy was watching television and drinking a cold beer when the evening news headlined, "Joey Provenzano, a member of Genovese crime organization, was killed yesterday." Andy leaned forward in his recliner and softly said, "I'll be damned." He thought to himself, *I knew John*

Colter's Code

was up to something. Now there's one less mobster preying on innocent people. The news continued to report that the shooting had occurred in the Green Mountains of Vermont when a lone gunman using a long-range sniper rifle shot Provenzano while he was skiing at the Stratton Mountain Ski Resort.

An interview with Windham County Sheriff Calvin Newfane followed Provenzano's picture on the screen. Newfane said, "We tracked the fugitive through the snow that evening, but blizzard conditions on the top of the mountain caused us to suspend the search. We resumed our hunt for the fugitive the next morning and scoured the mountain on snowmobiles, but we were unable to catch him. The suspect remains at large."

At Logan Airport, John changed his flight home to add a layover in Washington, DC. He wanted to make a special delivery. There, he boarded the red line subway train and changed at Metro Center to the blue line. At the fifth stop, John exited onto the Arlington Cemetery platform to begin his walk up Eisenhower Boulevard through the fields of white tombstones. He stopped to place a bouquet of dried flowers he had preserved from Amy's funeral on Jack's grave.

Tears rolled gently down John's cheeks onto the snow-covered grass. His throat tightened, he swallowed, and he softly spoke with resolve, "I know Amy is with you now. The two men who killed her,

Sal, and Joey Provenzano, celebrated in triumph when they walked out of the courtroom. They thought they were above the law. They believed their Mafia code reigned supreme, and their way of life was untouchable. They were wrong. Righteous judgment prevailed."

Then he asked himself, *Is my war with the Mafia over?*

A warm breeze arrived, bringing with it bright rays of sunshine piercing though the fluffy white clouds.

Made in the USA
Columbia, SC
03 October 2024